THE
FORGOTTEN SOUL
OF
Jasmine Peirce

ANGELINE V. NHERISSON

Order this book online at www.trafford.com
or email orders@trafford.com

Most Trafford titles are also available at major online book retailers.

Printed in the United States of America.

ISBN: 978-1-4669-5195-2 (sc)
ISBN: 978-1-4669-5197-6 (hc)
ISBN: 978-1-4669-5196-9 (e)

Library of Congress Control Number: 2012914408

Trafford rev. 08/09/2012

 www.trafford.com

North America & international
toll-free: 1 888 232 4444 (USA & Canada)
phone: 250 383 6864 ♦ fax: 812 355 4082

EAD IN THE CENTER OF what looks to be a decapitated
bridge, I find my lifeless body draped in vines, relying on the
paranormal skills of Harmony to bring me back to life. If nine
years ago as a child, someone had told me that my life would
turn out this way, I would have called this person a liar. My
mother worked hard to keep me in a safe environment or, for
a lack of a better term, a "safe house." That was the kind of
person my mother was always looking out for my best interest.
She toiled for a measly two dollar an hour to ensure I didn't
follow her path.

Although I was hated by most of my classmates, I always
thought the idea of growing into a responsible adult would be the
best way to redeem myself in society. A way to forget about the
misery that I went through as a child. I wanted to make sure my
childhood didn't follow me into adulthood. I'd think to myself,
if I could become the person society wants me to be, or at least
at a glance, I could gain the trust of my fellow classmates, who
spent their time making sure I found no happiness. I wanted to
be everything that comes with recognition and popularity. Maybe
a famous singer would do it for me even though I lack the skill
of singing or a famous actress like I have seen on American TV

or, if not, a successful doctor traveling the world to help those who couldn't afford good health care. I wanted to get involved in everything to impress the cynics. In my mind, all these things would show my capabilities to the world, and those who couldn't stand me would be envious of who I've become. That was my mind frame at the time, thinking that things would be that easy. Now that those dreams have been shattered by an assailant, I find myself lying under a bridge, hoping to get a second chance at life. I can't change the outcome of my chosen destiny; however, I can tell you the story of what brought me here, wandering in the afterlife at such an early age.

My name is Jasmine Pierce, and I once had fantasies of ways to escape this godforsaken town. Now being eighteen and dead, my fantasies have become my shadows, screaming to get attention from me. For years I've lived a broken life filled with pain, sleepless nights, and repeated nightmares that seem to have seized my youth. I started feeling very ill four years ago, and telling my new foster mom, Carole, that I was ill was not a good idea. I was so worried about making a bad first impression that worrying at some point became a major part of my illness. Carole Pierre had fourteen other orphans to worry about. My mission was to get these fourteen kids to like me and befriend them. They seem different from the other kids that I've met at the other houses. Carole's house, this new house, was my second chance to finally find a new group of people that I can relate to. I was hoping to find people who were searching for the same thing I was looking for. With a new town, I was hopeful that I will find a new beginning and forget what haunts me every day.

I wanted to do things to move forward with my life, but my health got in the way of that. My dreams, my wants, my needs all clashed before my eyes. I was worried about my future, and knowing my history of moving from foster home to foster home, I didn't really see where it was heading. There was no future. Every time I tried to move forward I found myself right back to where I started—ill, haunted, and traumatized.

With me being the new addition to the house, Carole now had fifteen kids to take care of, all on her own, in an overcrowded little house with three bedrooms. Each room held three kids. Even the living room and the dining room were turned into bedrooms. I was the new kid on the block. I didn't want to start out with a bad first impression. I was afraid of being judged by her if the wrong thing was said; when she told me that my room was a closet space near the bathroom I made no smart remarks about it. At this orphanage I was the oldest; the youngest was Ryan Cisco, who was only seven years old. Word in the house is his parents left him at the hospital shortly after birth and never came back for him. He has been with foster mom Carole since then. Ryan is a very frail-looking boy. At times I thought maybe Carole never fed him, but I've seen him eat, and he eats like a grown man. He eats everything and anything. Carole took good care of Ryan. I can tell that he was her favorite out of all of us. She gave much attention to him. She takes him out very often, even when there was very little money left to be spent, something that none of my ex-foster moms knew; caring for someone other than themselves. Thursdays and Fridays she takes him to the park, the movies and buys him ice cream. She took good care of Ryan especially. I love seeing how happy she makes him. If someone were to come and adopt Ryan, she would have a hard time coping with his absence.

Carole, my new foster mom, was a very genuine person who takes great pride in taking care of abandoned kids. I was in and out of foster homes since I was nine years old, and none of my ex—foster mothers were as genuine as she. I have gone through five foster moms prior to Carole, and all five of them never took notice of my existence unless of course the police starts showing up at the porch, saying, "Ma'am, is this kid . . . ?" And you know the rest of that story. Foster mom number one was overall a sad woman. The only thing she cared about was money, our charity money. The charity money given for the house was used for her personal needs. She was selfish and treated us carelessly. She never knew how to speak to us. Her famous line to us was, "No one wants you guys. Otherwise, you wouldn't be here eating food off the floor." She called the cops on me because I was coming home too late at night. I stood up for myself, unlike the other ones and she hated that. That's why she wanted me out of the house. To her I had no authority over anything because I was an orphan. I got physical with her at some point. Now I know getting physical with her was wrong, but at the time it felt right. She really didn't know how to talk to kids that were underage. Her language skills included profanity and only that. I was happy when she called the cops, and then it was off to the next foster home.

Foster mom number two was a different case of selfishness. An undercover alcoholic she was. Again she used our only source of funds, which was the charity money, for her own personal things. While we struggled for a meal every day, there she was buying expensive clothes for herself while we were wearing the same thing almost every day. For some of us, we were walking in sandals that were found on the streets; some of us even wore mismatched shoes to keep the sun from burning the soles of our feet. She was also an alcoholic. She often comes to the house with brown bags containing bottles of rum and other liquor. She buys extravagant things almost every time she goes out, starting with her alcohol. I know the little money she gets paid to stay with us was not that much to be going on shopping sprees every weekend while she left us alone in the house. She reminded me of my mother sometimes—well, most of the time I should say. They seem to have a habit of getting their lives taken over by alcohol and drugs. The other foster kids were afraid of her, but I wasn't. They were mute around her. The reason why? I don't know. God knows what she had done to them. They were kids of very few words, I must tell you. Lucky for me I didn't overstay my welcome. I never stay around long enough where I'm not welcome. The minute daylight hit I was gone. I was out of the house either for school or to steal with my older friends. I never gave her the chance to combat with my poor soul.

I reported foster mom number two to the owner of the orphanage, and they had her removed from the premises. I could not stand to be reminded of what my mother often did. I didn't want to remember my mother by only the bad. The owner of the orphanage found her bedroom closet stacked with bottles of wine, rum—you name it, she had it in her closet. Her closet was the nearest liquor store, except that she didn't buy them from a liquor store. She got them from merchants who were selling them in the streets. With some women, when you open their closets you find boxes of shoes; with her, it was nothing compared to that. Hers were filled with boxes of some opened and unopened bottles of liquor. Now I understand clearly why she was always moody and sassy when she gets up in the morning; she was having late-night drinking parties in her room by herself using our pity money. Sometimes it was extremely difficult for her to cook a proper meal for us. When she didn't cook at all during the day, her excuse was, "No donation came for us this month. Go out and find something to eat." Meanwhile, her breath smells like fresh-bought rum. For her, "go find food" meant begging the merchandisers for it. If they did deny me, I'd grab something and run away with it. The others just spent the day on an empty stomach. They weren't as clever as I was. She also made us go to bed earlier than the average kid. Our bedtime was six o'clock, a time when a normal family would be sharing stories at the dinner table about their days. With the sixteen of us, we were in bed while our stomach growled continuously. As the others forced themselves to sleep while starving, I was sneaking out of the house barefoot, walking the streets of Gonaive, Haiti, hanging out with my thieving friends who thought they had their lives all figured out. Being only ten at the time, I was a follower emulating their every move. They made me steal things for them, specifically food and cigarettes. Sometimes I would get hit by rocks being thrown at me when I run away without paying for the items. Ten was the new twenty for me. Even though I had a foster mom, I was doing everything on my own. I took care of myself when my mom should have been around for that. I was taking care of myself like a mother should. I was a ten-year-old kid who had to grow up really fast. It wasn't all turmoil with my mother. Through her

I learned how to take care of myself, moving from orphanage to orphanage.

The cops came and arrested her, and until after my death I still don't know what happened to her after they took her away in handcuffs. The next day when we woke up, we found this new old lady at the house making pancakes. Pancakes were wealthy people's breakfast. We didn't know much about it except that our stomach would love the taste of something like pancakes. We've only seen people eating it at fancy restaurants and on Saturdays, when we watched American TV. For some reason, we all wanted to try it. We wanted to know what was so good about it. "What do you guys want for breakfast?" We all shouted, "Pancakes!" It seems like we all had one thing in our mind, and that one thing was a good breakfast. Finally after Gabriel left, we were able to let loose. This new foster mom seemed nice, but I was sure she was putting up a front to show us that she's better than the previous foster moms that had stepped foot in the house. Well, at least the other kids were starting to talk. I was not around much to see them talking, but when I was around there was not much being said. Yes and nos were the only words it seems like they knew of. Now that Gabriel was gone, all hell broke loose. The new foster mom had revolutionized the house. Seeing the kids talking to one another at the breakfast table, I was ecstatic. The alcoholic had to leave in order for me to witness an amazing change. It's very funny how even in third-world countries we can have drug addicts and alcoholics. From watching movies I learned how to identify such people, and when I witnessed my mom die from such a thing, I knew then that she was one of those people. We suffer for food every day, and once little money comes around, some of us would rather spend it on things that have no value.

Believe it or not, foster mom number three was not too bad compared to the previous ones. The kids became completely different. They were talking, and even though sometimes getting food on the table was difficult, they were at least enjoying life more. By law, orphans were what we were; she didn't treat us no less. Similar to foster mom number two, I stayed there for two years.

When I turned twelve that's when my life turned to a complete nightmare. Even though foster mom number three was a nice woman, I was still sneaking out of the house on a nightly basis, stealing from those who themselves were struggling to feed their kids. At twelve I became a professional at stealing food from the merchants or from anyone who had food. I had been doing it for so long that I saw no wrong in doing it. The people I was hanging out with were troublemakers—kids who were seventeen years of age with no homes and no parents. They were the unknown. Being part of their crew, I also saw myself as an unknown. They were on the streets, stealing food, taking food out of the garbage to make it by each day. When I met them I thought sneaking out to hang with their circle was cool. I was twelve. Everything was cool to me, especially hanging out with the older kids. Smoking cigarettes made out of dried mango leaves was "cool." Everything preposterous that some of my older "friends" made me do was undeniably cool until one night I had to suffer the consequences of sneaking out of the house to meet them. I came to the point where I could not bear staying in Gonaives any longer. Walking the streets during daylight haunted my presence. My only choice was to leave foster mom number three. Leaving was the only way I could stop the shadow that followed my every step.

Foster mom number four, I stayed with her for just a week. She added the icing on top of my depression. Her depressing lifestyle took a toll on me after a week. She slept mornings, midday, and evenings. No matter what time of the day it was, she was in her room sleeping. She didn't really seem to care much about us or life itself. Behind those big dark eyes of hers was nothing but anguish. Her body language says, "I'm ready to give up on life." I packed my clothes and left. I needed to get away from the town that destroyed me. That little girl my mother had died the minute she witnessed her mother lying on the floor with foam coming out of her mouth. I can't help but think that I could have saved her if I had called someone in the neighborhood on time. After she passed, slowly, I became someone else. I came in contact with a dark world that took me away from all the things that I've dreamt of being. The police found me two days later after leaving the orphanage. They classified me as a runaway girl. I didn't see that as running away, not if I didn't have a home to begin with. I didn't have a family who was keeping track of me or anyone for that matter. My mom was the only person I had in my life, and before she died, I was the person she had in her life. If I did have a family, what happened to me seven years ago would have not occurred. Two days after walking on the road looking like a lost child, a police officer who was driving by stopped me and asked, "Shouldn't you be in school?"

"Don't worry about me," I said back to him.

The cop pulled over and started asking me questions, questions which I thought were irrelevant, questions like, "Where do you live?" For as long as I can remember I have not had a home since I was nine years old. Another one he asked me was, "How old are you?" I told him that I would be sixteen in three weeks. Although the questions were irrelevant, I answered him honestly, seeing that I had no reason to lie. He didn't believe me when I told him I was going to be sixteen years old very soon. It was mainly because I didn't really look my age. I was aging faster than my actual age. My eyes were as baggy and wrinkly as a forty-year-old woman. My nails looked like I've been working as a miner for years. With my torn-apart sandals, the officer looks at me up and down. What he sees was nowhere near flattering. My appearance didn't seem to fit his agenda, but I didn't care about his judgments anyway, so it was okay. Hate had played a major role throughout my life, so it was fine if he was repulsed by my appearance. I could never seem to get my hand around people who could teach me a thing or two about companionship. I was always an easy target for hate. So much was going through my mind when I got picked up by the officer. I was afraid that he was going to find a way to send me back to that town. I was afraid that he would recognize my face from when I use to run away with people's food without paying for them. I acted tough. I didn't want to go to jail though. I have heard a lot of bad things that could happen to me if I went. Some say the guards could beat me; the other thing that I was concerned about was having the guards forcing themselves on me. The older kids I used to hang out with tell me all sorts of things that they do to young girls, like forcing them to do things they didn't want to do. They used to tell me if I didn't steal things for them they were going to call an officer and have them arrest me.

The officer went on to ask more questions. "Do you have a home where I could drop you off at?"

"No, I do not have a home. I have a foster home, but I don't want to go there. I refuse to go back there," I told the cop.

"No pressure, I won't make you do anything you don't want."

"Thank you," I said to the officer.

"If you don't want to go there I'm sure I can bring you somewhere else where I can help you find someone you would like to stay with. Is that okay with you?"

I told him, "Take me far away from here." Asking to be far away wasn't good enough for me though. It wouldn't erase the destructive images in my head flashing back and forth. The only thing he could do for me if he really wanted to help me was to put me out of my misery. If he took that gun that settled on the side of his hip and put a bullet straight to my head, that would have been more help to me. Surprisingly, the officer was genuine. In the back of his car is where I was okay with the idea of maybe going far away. Start a new life. He drove me to the town next to Gonaives, Joule Ville. My older friends call it "the town of the rich." I was on my way to that town. He never told me that he was going to find me another foster home. Sitting in the back of his car, the scene outside was a little different from Gonaives. There were less kids walking barefoot on the streets. Some of them were wearing clean clothes and nice shoes, and most of them had an adult with them. So far my friends were right. It could pass for what they call "the rich town." People seemed courteous, waving hello to other passersby, another thing I haven't seen in a while. What I've seen are a lot of "Hey, get out of my sight, where's my money?" or "I will cut your throat." These are the words I'm familiar with. I'm not too familiar with friendly people or people who make a simple hello part of their days.

He found me a foster mother, and that's when foster mom Carole came into the picture. She was at the place where we went to. The moment our eyes collided with one another, there was an instant mother-daughter connection. She approached me. "Hi, how are you doing?" Looking like how I looked—scrubby, restless, wearing a pair of my mismatched sandals—I felt embarrassed to politely reply. Being the fresh girl that I was, I replied, "You don't know me," while rolling my eyes. She walked away, and the officer who was with me took a walk with her. They were whispering to one another as if they've known each other for a long time. I didn't know what they were talking about. However, my instinct said they were talking about me, saying nasty things just like the girls who sat in the back of me in art class used to, who knows. They both walked back toward me. The officer came and said, "Well, this lady will take good care of you for as long as you need her to. Don't worry about growing up too fast." And that's how Carole came into my life.

Again, I know you're asking yourselves this question: who is she, and how did she end up an orphan? Well, let me start out by introducing myself one last time. My name is Jasmine Pierce, and my soul wanders underneath the sky of Joule Ville, just waiting to explode. My soul will not rest until questions are answered. Shortly before turning sixteen, I was fortunate enough to be sent to live with Carole. Her being my foster mom was the best thing that had ever happened to me during my quest to find a new orphanage to call my home, an orphanage where I didn't have to deal with people who formed an opinion the second they laid their eyes on me. I was an orphan for a decade. I've watched families come in and out of Carole's house to pick their dearest child. Never have I been an option. Every time I see a man and a woman walking to our door, I was always excited and anxious to see who would be next in line. I stand in front of the door to see if I'd be their choice. Some of them walked right by me, avoiding my presence. I have been in and out of foster homes since I was nine years old. Never have I been the chosen one for any family. I was the chosen one for my mother, but my relationship with her was cut very short.

I remember when DSS came to get me as if it was yesterday. My mom was a drug addict, and everyone in the neighborhood knew it. There was not a drug out there that my mother wasn't familiar with. She even knew how to make some of them. Drinking was her kryptonite. For as long as I knew her, she was never completely sober. Her friends would come over and do the same things she does, which were snorting crack cocaine and drinking homemade rum.

It was a Saturday night when my mother and her friends were doing the usual routine—smoking tobaccos, drinking, and snorting homemade crack. At that time I was sitting on the couch watching my mother and her friends doing their thing, when out of nowhere my mother collapsed. I remember the music being so loud in the house. Watching my favorite cartoon show, *Jamina*, I rushed to her rescue, yelling out her name. On the floor my mother started to shake, foam coming out of her mouth and nose. Her eyes were bloodshot. Seeing that, I began to scream for help. Her friends screamed her name, "Liz, Madeline, wake up!" They shook her. No response. Her rapid shaking turned into silence. Her skin turned purple and frigid. When no response was heard from my mother, her friends grabbed their things and ran off, leaving me on the floor crying and screaming at my mother to wake up. I hit her, I shook her, I tried to make her sit down, but nothing. My mother died in my hands, and there was nothing I could do to save her. When I couldn't get her to get up, I ran around the neighborhood, screaming for someone to come help her. When aid finally came into the disarrayed house, she was gone, and I was never going to see her again. I never thought it was the last time I would ever see her again. If I knew, I would have learned to say better words. If I knew, I would have thought of something good to say to her before her shaking body became silent. My mother was only thirty-two when she died. She struggled to raise me by herself, and for that she is my hero. When the police came to take my mother's body away, the living room was a mess. Crack powder was all over the room, rum splashes on the floor. First clue that gave up the illegal activity going on in the house was the white powdery substance that covered my mother's face and the foam that was coming out of her mouth mixed with the crack that left a muddy trace. My mother could have been a great mother if she didn't do drugs, and her friends could have helped me save her had they not run away. The few hours during the days that she was sober, she cares for me like a mother should.

She tells me things like "I'm proud of you," "I hope you grow up to be nothing like me," and "Everything you do is perfect." Even when I act like a snob I was perfect to her. She did give me some great motherly advice for when I was old enough to be on my own. Let's face it; my mother had flaws that I couldn't stand. She had friends who used her to get high. My mother worked really hard to keep food on the table for the two of us, sometimes even for the friends who left her to die on the floor. Sometimes it kills me, knowing that if I had ran outside for help earlier, she and I would still be well alive today, but the past is the past. I must learn to move forward and forget about those who have hurt me.

See, I'm not an orphan by choice. When my mother passed away, she had no family members to live me with. It was just her and I; it's always been. With no will left from her it was just like saying, "Throw her in with the rest of them," and I was thrown with the rest of them, fending for myself every day.

If my mother was still alive the things that have happened could have been prevented. For the short time I've lived with her she kept me grounded. She always made sure that my schoolwork was done on time and made sure I had the things a nine-year-old girl should have even if it meant working extra hours. She worked ten hours a day in a clothing factory, making only two dollars an hour. Sometimes she'd come home with her fingers poked in many places by needles, complaining how much pain she was in. She didn't have a mansion to raise me in or money to pay for a nanny to take care of me after I come back from school or had money to buy me fancy things, but she raised me well for a good eight years. She raised me well to the point where I could wash my clothes, stay in by myself, and wait for her to come home to make dinner for me. Occasionally when she was too tired, I'd cook for her. She and I helped each other. Being nine years old, she taught me how to do everything. If it was not for her drug habits, none of the things that were done to me would have happened. We could have still been in that little house helping one another to get by each day, or I could have been on my way getting ready for the college life or even working with her side by side in that clothing factory, who knows. Life is unpredictable. If she were around, I know one thing for sure—I would not be weeping over my dead body right now. I remember one time when I was seven years old in second grade; I got so tired of this girl making me cry all the time in front of my classmates I decided to tell her about it. That day, instead of me taking the school bus, she walked me to school and headed straight into the classroom, fuming, livid about what she had learned. Right when she got into the classroom, she asked me, "Baby girl, which one of these girls was making fun of you?" I sobbingly pointed out exactly who she was. She didn't care that the teacher was around. She went up to her and said, "If you ever make my girl cry, let alone touch her in any way, shape, or form, I will come back here and show you how it feels to be made fun of in front of all your little friends here, understand!" Faith was her name. She shook her head and said quietly to my mother, "Yes." My mother made her cry. I enjoyed watching her tearing up. I was glad that it was not me this time around. I will never forget that day. What she did for me I consider to be a great mother–daughter moment. Faith never dared to make fun of me again. In fact, she became my only friend in third grade. I don't know why they called her Faith. Her personality didn't fit her name.

Every night I wonder if my mother made it to heaven or not. I wonder if she's in heaven watching over my soul, which has not yet been taken over. Overall, there was never anything special about us two as beings. Everything about our lives was the way it shouldn't be.

This orphanage seemed somewhat okay compared to the ones I came from, but the kids were mean to a very high extent. If it was four years ago, I would have knocked them out one by one. I didn't have the energy to make them part of my problems. When I went to bed I was having nightmares, when I went to school the kids were picking on me, and when I came home I couldn't be at peace because of the constant screaming around the house. They were so alive, full of energy, running around the orphanage like it was their birthplace. Often they were arguing with one another, especially Rodney and Marc; they were males who fought like cats. If they weren't fighting about a static television that you could barely see anything from then it was about Marc wearing Rodney's jeans or shirts. I silently thought of them as the couple of the house; they fight like a married couple. Their fighting triggers flashbacks that couldn't be controlled. They reminded me of that man I had to fight. I was Marc. I got discouraged quickly after realizing I stand no chance.

Marc was not as rough or tough as the guy that forced himself on me, yet he sure knows how to put up a good fight. Marc was a chunky little thing whose language was really hard to understand. Marc told me that he came here from the Dominican Republic when he was seven years old with his aunt. His aunt got with the wrong people, and that's how he ended up here. When he tries to speak, the French language sounds odd. He pronounces *moi*, like "me-ahh." When he fights Rodney and wins, he runs around the house, screaming, "quoi, quoi" repeatedly, the meaning of which I don't know. Only Rodney knew his language. Marc was a twelve-year-old boy who couldn't read neither in his language nor in French. In the Dominican Republic he never went to school. He stayed with his uncle and helped with fixing cars. Anything that needed to be fixed around the house Marc says he could fix. Of course none of us believed him. When he did break things around the house he'd bring them to Carole. His best friend in the house was Rodney, of course, who didn't even know the first thing about speaking Spanish but understood his broken French. Somehow, in some weird way, they understood each other very well. I was jealous of that. They had something that I wished I had—a true friendship.

In the house everyone seemed to have someone they clicked with. As for me I was still getting used to the idea that this place might be the place for me till I turn eighteen or till someone comes and adopts me. Nicole was best friends with Marlene. They were around the same age, thirteen. Nicole was just a couple of months older than her. Every time I looked at them I felt like they were whispering about me. Again it could be my subconscious deceiving me. No one knew me or has seen the horrible things that I have gone through, yet they formed an opinion. As far as how they got here, I didn't know. I didn't get the chance to get to know them. Shortly after arriving at the house, they got adopted by some rich family. They were a nice couple. They told Marlene and Nicole that they were going to be part of their family now. They were lucky to get adopted by the same family. These two were inseparable.

At night I had nightmares, nightmares that were repetitive and true. I'd have nightmares of the faceless man who forced himself on me seven years ago. The nightmares were of him coming back to do the same thing again. In my reverie he was always chasing me just like he did when he forced himself on me. Often he'd catch me, and occasionally I'd escape him. As I scream for help he would vanish, and when I was weak to do so, I would see him on top of me with his shirt covering my mouth. The nightmares were different each night about the one man chasing me. I see him laughing at me as I scream, "No! Get off me!" Once he was done, he would leave me stranded, crying with no one in sight to get help from. I would wake up in the middle of the night with tears running down my cheeks, with the same thing playing in my mind reiteratively. This was not a movie; it was a reality that I could never escape. It was haunting me in my sleep. Every time I see a guy walking by or sitting next to me, I'd have flashes of it. Men had become the devil to me, and I couldn't stand the idea of being around them. Being near them just triggers the memories. Alone by myself, I felt as if I was being watched by the faceless man. When I was alone, I was never really alone. He was my shadow, laughing because he got away with committing such a crime. That assailant left me traumatized. He was an image that was difficult to get rid of.

I never had skills when it comes to making friends or keeping friends. I'm eighteen years old now, and I can't tell you if I've had a true friend, but I can tell you that I made a lot of enemies instead. Making enemies was my curse. At the orphanage, I had enemies, and at school I had even more of them. Everywhere I went, people would look at me with disgrace. Going to a new school, starting fresh, it was my goal to make friends, especially in a "rich" town such as Joule Ville.

"I'm driving you to school on your first day?" Carole asked which was a first. No foster mother had ever asked to drop me off to school before. It's either I had to take the bus or walk miles and miles away to the school. I was surprised. I really wasn't expecting that.

I learned something about her that day. She can talk. There was never a silent moment with her. "Why are you so quiet? Judging by the expression on your face every day, I can see that you hold so much in."

"Oh no, I'm fine."

"There's something you're not telling me, Jasmine."

"What am I not telling? There's nothing to tell," I said to her. I was glad the school was nearby. Otherwise, I'd have to find some way to answer her remedial questions. Before I knew it we were at the school. Just when I was about to open the door of the car, Carole says to me, "Just because I'm not your real mother does not mean I'm not your mother."

"Okay," I told her.

"If I'm here to take care of you guys that means I am your mother. Mothers take care of their children. Do not hesitate to come and talk to me."

"Okay," I replied again.

Everything she said was real. She cared about us, all thirteen of us. Within the three weeks I lived there I saw rare things, like

Carole treating all thirteen of us with respect. In all my years of being in orphanages I came to the realization that all foster mothers were all the same—mean, selfish, overbearing, and with issues. I was wrong. Carole was nothing like that; she was a fifty-seven-year-old Haitian woman whose heart had nothing but pure love and generosity.

Walking through the corridors of the high school, my first thought was, *What a jungle.* Everyone kept staring at me as if I was infectious. In class they made me uncomfortable with their eyes cornering me. Going to lunch, everyone had a clique that they sat with. I looked around to see who I can sit with. Their body gestures say, "Get away from me, you freak." I didn't want to show people I had no friends, so I took my lunch and made my way to the bathroom to eat it. The bathroom was not the most pleasant place to eat your lunch at; it wasn't even the most pleasant thing to use. It smelled and had roaches crawling around. The bathroom screamed unflushed urine and defecation. It was not the most pleasant place to be in—period. The size of the roaches crawling around it tells its story. That roach-infested bathroom became my cafeteria. As time progressed, I became immune to it.

During lunch I'd sit in there for a good forty-five minutes, hoping that the girls would stop talking about the new girl in school, the new girl being me. One of those girls accidentally saw me eating my lunch there. She didn't pay much attention, as I stopped chewing my mouth. I think she disregarded the fact that I was eating and thought I was really using the toilet. The bathroom had a strong odor; however, the girls didn't seem to care much about it. They turned the bathroom into the gossiping room. During my first day at the school, I heard one of the girls who was brushing her hair say something about me. "Have you seen that new girl? What was she wearing? She looks hideous. She looks homeless." Little did I know that she was going to sit right in front of me in French class. She spent the whole period whispering to her friends about how gross I was. Gosh, how I was uncomfortable. Even I had begun to second-guess myself. The first day of school was nothing like I imagined. Wanting to start fresh, the day was not in my favor. My first day in school, I had already made an enemy when I was supposed to be making friends. My appearance didn't give me a chance.

Once school was over, Carole was already at the entrance in her rattling car, waiting for me. That car was as tired as I was. It was rusty and covered with dust. The headlights were broken and hanging from the side, and the bumper was hanging down, making a dragging sharp noise when she drives. When I got into the car, Christina was already in the backseat, lying against the backseat in a hiding position, clenching her body. I could understand why she was hiding; she was a pretty girl who didn't want to be seen in the damaged vehicle. Carole was proud of driving that car. That car got us everywhere we wanted to go. Christina was one of my housemates. She was fifteen years old at the time, a little closer to my age. She was a freshman at Judem High, the same school I was attending. Funny, I didn't even see her at school that day. Something that set Christina apart from the rest of us was her image; she didn't look like an orphan. How she ended up in a foster home was a mystery at first. She had hazel-brown eyes, skinny, had long soft brown hair, and had flawless dark skin that resembled Dove chocolate, my favorite candy bar. She had a glow to her that I've never seen on anyone else. Her attitude was what kept her from ever getting adopted. She was better than everyone else in the house according to her. She was a pretty girl with an ugly heart. What's the point of being pretty if your heart is ugly?

"So, Jasmine, how was your first day at school?" Christina asked. My day sucked. I hate everyone in my class. I want to shove that girl against the lockers for talking shit about me at French class today. And I hate you and everyone else, 'cept for Carole, of course. Well, that's what I wanted to tell her. Can't a girl fantasize? I simply responded by saying, "Fine." She sits in the back of the car, and what do you know—she was brushing her hair. Typical. I saw her as the little doll my mother gave me when I was a little girl. "Monica," I named it. Christina resembled Monica very much. If you were walking on the street and saw her you would think she was rich. A spoiled child she acted like. Back at the orphanage it was a different story.

As always the house was crowded. It's even more crowded after school. Everyone's home. I had assumed that I was not going to make it in the house. It was the kind of place I needed to be in. A place where I can sleep is what I wanted. With Carole's I learned to cope with a noisy home. That house was the closest thing I had to a home.

Every day I woke up, my body felt abnormal. When I thought I was going to feel well the next day, I felt worst. After school my room was where I'd go straight into. In my room I can try to relax and avoid the noises in my head and the noises that came along with the house. Try or not, I could never escape my head. Flashes of my nightmares come as it pleases, night and day. At school, at the park, alone—those nightmares followed me everywhere.

It's been a long three months of being at the orphanage, a home where I was beginning to create myself. The nightmares settled in my head, but little by little I learned to avoid them. I was no longer the new girl at school, but still I was the target for people to poke fun of, especially for Daphne François. She sits behind me in French class, pulling my thinning hair, flicking it with her pencil. That was her job, basically to make an entertainment out of me. When she didn't have her American magazines I was her source of amusement. My own body was poking fun at me wherever I go. I could never get a break even in my own head.

Christina was the soon-to-be it girl at school. No one poked fun at her. At school she didn't know me. She ignores me when she sees me. She was afraid of people finding out that we shared the same home also. That was fine with me. I didn't trouble myself over if she speaks to me or not. She avoids me and I did the same. Girls hated her and the boys wanted her. Daphne couldn't stand Christina. They both hated one another. In Math class if Daphne wasn't making fun of my appearance then she was talking to her friends about how much she hated Christina.

I don't even see what people see in her. She's not even that pretty," Daphne says as she twirls her brown hair. Oh Christina was prettier than her and she could not stand it. Her boyfriend wanted Christina and she couldn't have that.

Christina—"manipulation" should have been her name—used her boyfriend to make her mad. Often Christina flirted with Daphne's boyfriend and he loved it. He was too stupid to see that Christina was only playing games with him to get even with her. It was an ongoing war between the two. At school Daphne was the rich girl. She had money, the chauffeur, the beauty, and style. Everyone wanted a piece of her. She was soon-to-be the ex-it girl 'cause Christina's thirst for popularity was taking over. At home Christina was a different person. She turns into this little girl who cries very often. She goes home, and her room suddenly becomes her friend from 3:00 p.m. till the next day she wakes up for school. She seldom ate dinner with us. That's what I noticed toward the beginning of my stay. A question could never be asked about her life. Her response would always be, "It's none of your business." and then she slams the door right in your face.

In front of people she was Monica—strong, beautiful, and flawless; behind closed doors she was fragile. One night I went to use the bathroom, and I heard a crying noise coming from her room. It appears as if someone was suffocating her. She was squeezing the pillow on her face, trying to block the devastating noise coming out of her mouth. All I know from sharing the same orphanage is that deep down inside she's just as miserable and secretive as I was. Inside her head there was a world that was being wicked to her just like me. You can't have best of both worlds, can you now?

The world I knew of was wicked to me, and the world I tried to hide from was far from perfect. I was filled with hate. Hate is what I've grown to know; after my mother died, my idea of loving died with her. She was the only person whom I loved. She was the only one I had to love.

Five months passed by since my arrival at the Nelson orphanage. There wasn't much change going on. We went through the same routine always. We all wanted to be with a family. No one came for the thirteen of us left. We've seen couples come by to check but left empty-handed. Christina gets second looks. Because of her attitude they reconsider their choices. Seeing someone new in the house, she either takes their bags and goes to her room with it or asks them for money. When they refuse to give her money, she'd throw their wallet at them. She was very disrespectful to newcomers. She expected to get everything she asked for. Carole was a nice lady, but none of them wanted to be in the house.

We all wanted to be part of a family, but instead we were all wandering. It's even more depressing when they all go to the park. They'd come home not wanting to do anything, feeling depressed and sorry for themselves. In the house they only had each other to rely on. Sometimes Carole's comfort wasn't enough. While they had each other to rely on, I had myself, and I was okay with that. I couldn't worry about them. Too many changes were taking place in my body.

My body was getting weaker and weaker every day. I woke up one morning with blood coming out from my nose. My pillow was semidrenched with the red fluid. My body was changing, not for the better but for the worse. I didn't know how to talk to anyone or who to talk to about what was going on with me. The more I tried to keep my appearance a secret, the more people began to see there was something drastically wrong with me. I lived in fear of dying every day. There was something new happening to me, and I realized that every morning. Waking up in the middle of the nights vomiting, with my body feeling like I've been standing in the middle of a fire for days were part of my problem. At night, I was getting fevers that couldn't be contained by drinking ice-cold water or by putting cold towels over my forehead. Since Haiti is known for voodoo, I started thinking that maybe my mother had gotten on the wrong side of some people, and they may have casted a wicked spell on us, a spell that determines our short time here on Earth. These could all be possibilities for why our lives turned out this way. For the past months, I went from being 130 pounds to a staggering 100 pounds. I was shedding pounds without even trying. After being a target for my weight at school, I did like losing the weight, but why was I losing it? I was sicker than I had originally thought. I wanted this to all go away. This ongoing illness was rare. I lived nine years with my mother, and I was never this sick. Why now?

As I fixed myself to have some breakfast with the other kids at the house, all of the sudden I felt the urge to regurgitate. With my hand covering my mouth, I still couldn't keep myself from regurgitating food mixed with partial blood. Carole, who was cooking breakfast, ran to the bathroom to make sure that I was okay. She took a wet towel and put it over my head to bring down the fever that took over my body.

"Your body is hot! Jasmine, what is going on with you? You can stay home today," she says to me.

Walking back to my room, the other kids stared, shouting how much of a baby I was. If they knew and felt how much pain I was going through I'm sure they would reconsider feeling that way toward me. "All of you guys need to shut up. Get your backpacks and go," Carole said to them. I didn't know the other kids well enough to start judging them; all I knew is that they had no compassion in their hearts. When you're an orphan there's no such thing as companionship. It's rare to find. When I first came into the house they were getting along well with one another. They all had someone who they were friends with. The more time they spent at the Nelson orphanage, the more aggressive they get. They all had some grudge against one another, especially for Abigail and Shauna; they were often eyeballing one another at the dinner table. I was confused, lost, trying to understand what was going in their head. I tried to figure them out to avoid being in conflict with them.

At times they were mute, standing or sitting altogether in a half dining room and a half bedroom to eat. I guess seeing families come in and out of the house and leaving empty-handed could be part of their mood swings. The only time they spoke to each other was when they were fighting. This bewildered me. It didn't really faze them at the breakfast table when they saw me gagging.

They all looked at me with this disgusting look on their faces, like I was ruining their appetite. Right when Shauna saw that I was about to throw up, she got off the breakfast table and left for school, murmuring about how this household changed into a thing of disturbance since my arrival.

They were all young children who acted like the world revolved around them, especially when people came for a visit. I remember this incident when this newlywed couple, who's been donating to the orphanage long before I came in, came for a visit to see how everything was going. They also had in mind to adopt Christina, I've been told by Carole. They had in mind for a while that Christina would be a nice addition to their growing family. They came greeting everyone. Anise, who acts as if she was the chosen one, decided it was a good idea to throw rice at them in an effort to make them notice her. Carole could never contain her. She acted bizarre whenever people came over; it didn't matter who it was. The other kids running out of their rooms surrounded them with embarrassment, not love and appreciation. Ryan took his partially ripped shirt off, throwing it at them. The couple stayed around for an hour, playing with them. At first it was weird how they showed no sadness toward the other kids' behavior. Looking at them from my room, I thought they were okay with their behavior. Upon leaving, they hugged everyone and said their good-byes. Since that day the couple never came back, not even for Christina. They used to send letters; the letters stopped coming. That couple was the last couple I saw coming to the house. Christina was destroyed after it sunk in that the couple was never coming back for her. The repeated embarrassments had given them a change of plan, and Christina was no longer part of that plan. As much as I hated it her, it saddened me to see how hurt she was when she realized they were not coming back for her.

Anyway, let's continue with the story. Despite being in so much pain and not being able to keep anything down, I was happy to know that I had parental permission to avoid school that day. It was a first. Since my mom died, I had never had someone tell me that it was okay to stay home for being sick. The other foster mothers didn't care what condition I was in. The minute the sun hit, it's pack up your things and get out of the house.

Carole took me down to my room and asked if she could make some soup for me. It was always a struggle to eat what she cooks. My throat would not accept it. Her food often goes in the trash barrel right after she serves it. I couldn't give them to the other kids because they didn't want to eat anything from me. They would rather starve themselves to death. Shauna has said that to me once before, and if one says or does one thing the others follow. My sore throat never goes away. Sometimes it takes a toll for the worst, and sometimes I faintly feel it. For the past year my sore throat has been consistent. It never went away completely. It was hard to take anything in, even most soups. Anytime anything touches my throat, there was a burning sensation that would stay around for hours.

Carole's bread soups were always good and refreshing, but consuming them was a battle. Whenever I force myself to consume it, I'd feel strong, alive, and rejuvenated. When I'm starving from days without eating solids, even though I knew the consequences of swallowing, I'd drink her soups like there was no burning pain. She took my temperature and it was 102 degrees. She asked to take me to the hospital, but I refused. I hated the hospital. When I was seven years old, my mother took me to the hospital for a sprained ankle, and it was recommended that I have surgery done to the leg. Because my mother didn't have money for the operation, they wrapped my leg in a cloth and sent my mother and I home. "Her leg will heal itself in time. She's young," said the doctor after learning that my mom couldn't pay for the procedure. Before learning that my mother couldn't pay for the operation, they rushed me to a hospital bed, telling her that my leg will get infected if the surgery wasn't done immediately. In my world there were three kinds of people—the rich, the poor, and the orphans. Before I fell into the orphan category, my life was based on my mother's struggles to provide for her daughter. I spent weeks in pain and in hunger, couldn't walk, and couldn't help my mom with the house chores. She had to stay home to take care of me while I was sick. Ever since then, hospitals became my enemy. Why? Because they bring your hopes up, and once they learn you're not part of the rich community, they tell you to go home. Living with my mother, I would always hide my sickness to avoid going to the hospital for two reasons—I didn't want her to stop working because of me, and I didn't want her to feel like she couldn't take care of her daughter. She hated not being able to pay for the procedure. I could see it in her face. At that hospital I also made a promise to myself that I was never to allow myself get sick again. She never knew when I was sick. I was good at keeping things to myself.

Carole took great care of me; she was the next best thing to a mother. Unlike the others, she didn't feel I was any sort of obligation to her. She dedicated her time when I was in dire need.

"If you still feel like this by tomorrow, I'm taking you to the hospital."

"I just need rest, that's all."

Come the next day I was feeling much worse. I could not sleep; nightmares of that man forcing himself on me remained. I couldn't even doze off in class without having the man in my head make a mockery of me. It was a game to him. I was this poor little shrinking girl that got chased every night by him; he would have his way with me no matter what direction I went in. I go out and I see kids my age having the time of their lives, playing with their friends, doing what they love to do. As for me, I had no friends, even when I was living with my mother. They picked on me because of my look. Some called me the ugly duckling, Ms. Stick, or, my favorite, "skeleton." My name was irrelevant to the ones who saw me as an opportunity for laughter. When it comes to socializing with friends, I didn't know what it meant.

School was hell, and even in my room I couldn't escape the voices in my head. Wherever I was, the word "safe" had no meaning to it. A week has gone by since I tried to avoid Carole from taking me to the hospital. I had done nothing but skip school. Some days I stay in school, and other days I just take a different route immediately after Carole turns her car around. I was sick and tired of the tortures at school. The grayer I look, the more fun they made of me. They constantly picked on parts of my body that were unappealing to them, which was everything, I guess. For every part they didn't like, they would poke it, either with their pencils or their fingers. Some of them were scared to touch me, so their pencils or pens were what they used on me. I was so sick of still being seen as the new girl that I prayed every day for a new girl to open that entrance door to take my place. Maybe then they would leave me alone. What I hated the most in school was that most of the students were ignorant and apathetic toward my feelings. My teachers called me retarded because I could never focus to pass tests. Whenever a test was assigned, I got nervous, itchy, and sweaty; and by the time I was done with scratching myself and asking to use the bathroom, the time would be up. For all the teachers, we had thirty minutes to take a test. Once time was up and pencils were down, you couldn't do anything else. When I fail a test, the teacher throws me out of the class while others pass by, calling me names. For the popular ones who were thrown out of class, it was a time for them to socialize with the passersby, but if you were like me, standing outside was a time to get papers thrown at your face. Kids would pass by and pinch me and saw no wrong in doing that. When I speak to my teachers about the students hitting me and calling me names, they'd tell me, "There's nothing I could do about the students' feelings toward you."

Talking to the teachers was like talking to my former foster moms—they never acknowledge anything I say. They never knew my name either. Emanuel Leon, who sat two chairs away from me in art class, calls me "that girl" or addresses me with "hey." It's like I didn't have a name. If I had a voice of my own, I would stand up and tell them what I imagine in my head. "My name is Jasmine Pierce, and if you can't say it then don't call me at all!" I learned all of their names the first day I came to class. They spend way too much time making spitballs to throw at me and too much time pulling on my oversized shirts in the hallway. To them I was nothing but simply a way to make their lives less miserable.

In perspective, skipping school has its rewards. Circling Judem Valley High was one way of skipping school. Being new in the town, I didn't really know where to go until one day I challenged myself to take a different route. I walked miles on a rainy day and came across this bridge, the bridge that is now helping to bring me back to life. The bridge seemed like no one has walked its path yet. Underneath, the bridge was covered with green grass, spiraled branches, and vines that made up its unique climate. The bridge was untouched; it was rich and pure. I felt lucky to stump unto this peculiar environment. Standing underneath the bridge I felt like I was home again with my mother, the sober one, the one that would go all the way to make sure that nobody dared to put their hands on the one she loved. Finally, I felt like I was home again. Under the bridge I felt serene. There, the word "safe" had meaning. That was the one place I could hide from anyone, including the man controlling my nightmares. There he was never going to find me. For the first time in a while I slept without being interrupted by that man. My body took a course for the better every time I was under that bridge. That bridge became my place for serenity and healing. The only sad thing about this place was I couldn't take it with me to the orphanage.

Under that bridge, which I called Harmony, I had friends, friends that could fly, friends that swam, and friends that weren't afraid to sit next to me, friends that didn't think I would give them rabies. These friends were animals of many kinds. Birds, rabbits, squirrels, and, my favorite of course, the swans that were swimming up and down the river that ran seamlessly. These friends came in packs. Struggling to eat my buttered sandwich, I found friends that I could share my lunch with. It was great to see them fighting over my roughened bread. If I couldn't eat it, I was glad that I was no longer throwing the food in the barrel. Someone other than me could enjoy it, and that someone was the animals.

When I was at the orphanage with Carole, I was ill, even when she tried her best to help me. I couldn't save myself from regurgitating at night, I couldn't eat, I had high fevers; but when I was with Harmony I felt like a new person living among the wealthiest. The swans understood me, the squirrels were my friends, and the birds sang to me. I was undeniably happy sitting under Harmony. Harmony was heaven-sent. Staring at the clear blue sky, with clouds white as snow appearing in the shape of a swan, a bird, or a squirrel, there was no way I was going to win best attendance in school. However, being in that moment, I was making some fun memories of my own. Nothing was better than here, especially when it came to school. At school I had no one. But with Harmony I had beautiful friends who loved me just as I was. The squirrels were speaking to me. I thought I was hallucinating. I could have sworn the squirrels were talking to me. I rubbed my eyes to see if I was just seeing things. I wasn't. I could really understand them. They were all talking at once. They were saying things like, "Welcome!" And all of the sudden the birds and the swans were also talking. I couldn't believe it. Someone besides me needed to know about this. Who could I trust to tell of this amazing story? And if I did tell someone about this then they would know about Harmony, and I couldn't risk that. Harmony was and is my hideaway from the demonic world.

Less and less I was showing up to school. Christina noticed my absence, and at home she was giving me the attitude. Usually at home I'd get a forceful "Hi, how was school?" Since I've discovered Harmony it's been different. She would roll her eyes at me. At school we always had the same lunch period together. If we didn't see each other in the hallway then lunch was the place we would catch a glimpse of one another. We never hung out at school nor did we hang out at home. According to her I would crimp her style if she was seen in public with me. She was afraid to be seen talking to me, let alone letting people know that we shared the same overcrowded orphanage. It would "mortify" her. I never understood clearly why she was so angry at me.

She was finicky when it comes to her acquaintances. She hung out with the cheerleaders, who thought they ran the school and the whole soccer crew. Most of them were her friends because of the person she perceives herself as. If only they knew the person I knew. Some days I chose to skip Harmony and headed straight to class after Carole had dropped us off at school. Christina and I weren't the best roommates in the world. She was cold and heartless the entire time I lived under the same roof as her. I can remember asking Christina if I could sit with her at lunch one time, and her response to me was, "You wish!" I really didn't want to spend my first day at the school eating my lunch in the bathroom. It didn't hurt to ask, but it hurts getting that answer from her. I thought about my real friends while eating my lunch in the bathroom. I thought as the long days passed, she'd be accepting of me. It's been three months sharing the same house, and she still was the same heartless person I met when I first went to the house. I sat in the toilet forcing myself to eat lunch. I was starving. I couldn't keep anything down. When I was not at Harmony I was empty. I felt like I was not needed when I was not there. Sitting in the toilet, all I could hear was the girls talking about me. This one girl started the conversation by saying, "Hey, that ugly fat girl is back. I saw her walking in the hallway head bowed. Bitch looks hideous!"

The other one went on to say, "Oh that girl. I thought she was out sick. She looks so weird. She looks really sick. I think I'm going to talk to her when I see her at math class."

Another girl went on to say, "You talk to her, don't talk to me!" By now they must know that I am in the bathroom listening. Three good months had gone by. These girls were nothing but pure evil. Their lives must have been pretty poor for them to come to school making fun and gossiping about me to make their lives less painful than mine. In school most of us struggles for something. Some of us are professionals at hiding struggles. Take Christina as a prime example of that. Some of us worry about what dinner will consist of, some of us worry about not being raised by their biological family, and some of us worry about if they will live to see the next day. Take me for instance. I went to bed worrying about if I'm going to live to see another day again. Kids at school pry on the weak and ill to occupy their current voids. My existence seems to bother them.

Some people saw me as the girl who wears the same outfit over and over again or the "skeleton" girl or the girl with the frizzy hair. I was simply those things they say I was. As weeks turned to months, I started believing in the things they thought of me. Maybe I *was* those things they say I was. I was just too caught up in feeling sick all the time that I couldn't see it. I've never done harm to any of them. Only in my head I'd fantasize of how I wanted to hurt them, just like they hurt me. That's as harmful as I get. People have done more to me than I even think of doing to them. I spent my days and my nights thinking about that night when I got my innocence taken away from me, and I wish I never snuck out of that orphanage house. If I had stayed in the house like the other ones, this would have never happened to me. I would have still retained my innocence, and the flashbacks that kept me from sleeping at night would have been something I would block my face from when watching horror movies. But in my case, I experienced every bit of that horror. Everything was real.

The night that man ran after me, yes, I was starving of hunger. I had some energy to run for my life, but still he caught me. He tore my shirt apart. When I tried to fight him off, I was beaten repeatedly. When I refused to give him myself, I was spit on. I tried to bite him, but he knocked me unconscious with his fist. He was a monstrous man who looked like he was hungry for girls like me, vulnerable and lost. I didn't have an owner, so I became an easy target, walking on an empty street in the middle of the night, searching for a way out, a better existence. I was his victim, if not one of his victims. The neighborhood was packed with homeless adults who thought they were untouchable. At thirteen I also thought I was untouchable, and look at what happened to me. Because of that man, the thought of boys disgust me. I see a nice young man and all I could think about is that man. In my head I see them as that man who ruined my life six years ago. I was the victim of a monster who scarred me for life, even as I lie on the ground dead.

After discovering the bridge I was under the suspicion that Christina knew that I was avoiding school. I wasn't trying to disregard school. I loved school. It was a step toward creating a "future." I went to school with the same people poking fun at me, and when I did skip school it was mainly because I was trying to avoid the people who were discouraging me.

While eating my lunch in the bathroom, I heard Daphne's friends talking about how she had lost it all. One of Daphne's closest "friends" said that her parents were sleeping in different beds. In this school if you wanted gossip, the bathroom was the place to get it. I heard it all, from breakups to pregnancies. There was always a live show going on in the bathroom. When they weren't talking about me I found their conversations somewhat entertaining.

It was funny how they all poke fun at me when most of them had problems of their own. The next day, while having my lunch, I heard Daphne bursting in tears and mumbling to herself about her parents, saying things like "What am I going to do?" I overheard her saying she was going to apply for a job at a boutique after school to help her mother out. She spoke as if she was speaking to someone, yet there was no one in sight but her and I. It was something I often do, talking to myself as if I'm talking to someone. She wanted to help her family get through whatever it was they were going through. That's what I gathered from what she was whispering to herself. That was an unselfish side of her that I saw that day. It's so funny how karma works. She once said that working was for poor people. I got off the toilet and pointed my ears to listen more. She saw me and left the bathroom, pretending I was not there. I had two guesses of what's wrong with her—either her parents were getting a divorce or her father, the breadwinner of the house, lost his job. Divorcing is not as bad as losing a job in Haiti; losing a job means everyone has to start chipping in. How can one be okay from having maids doing everything for them then waking up one day and have all that be taken away? Reality hits hard. If I were her I would be worried about that too, considering how much she likes to brag about her rich life. Her father was a successful surgeon who decides who is rich enough to get his treatments, and her mother basically stayed at home spending his money. Sometimes Daphne would walk in class with the newest designer bag or shoes from America, bragging about how her father had her clothes imported straight from the land of money. Going to America was every student's dream. Daphne was the only one from school lucky enough to go as she pleases; her parents went on vacations there. She bragged to us about how in America only the rich lived there, and it was the place for everything entertaining and more according to her. America was one of the reasons why she had so many friends. Her friends thought if they stuck around enough then she'd take them one day to America. She made it seem so easy to get into America. If you were rich or hang out with the rich then you were lucky enough to get into America. The only reason she was in that school was because she couldn't get into the top private Catholic schools and not because her father couldn't afford it. She didn't meet their requirements. Judem Valley High wasn't for stupid people; it was a public school for the parents who couldn't afford private school for their kids. It was a school dedicated to bring out the best in people, but the teachers changed its definition. The teachers had favorites, and at times they were mean to the nonfavorable.

After her rich lifestyle stopped, her followers, or what you may call her crew, disappeared. They were no longer sitting with her at lunch. Some of them were seen with Christina and the soccer players. They all took a different direction after seeing that she was no longer wearing the fancy garments or when her chauffer stopped driving her to school. Daphne became a regular in the bathroom. Since I've been to this school never have I seen Daphne show any sympathy toward anyone else. When she saw me throwing up in the bathroom, she looked at me and asked if I was all right. Things must have been really bad at her house for her to feel the need to be nice to the homeless. Many times during her rich spoiled days she'd call me "the homeless girl." I was the homeless girl that did favors for her during class. "Hey, homeless girl, can you pick up my pencil?" "Homeless girl, can you give me some white line papers?" And because I was trying to make friends, I would respond to her. It was "homeless girl this" and "homeless girl that." In that short moment I didn't see any of that "I'm better than you" look from her.

Not being with Harmony for so long, all I wanted to do was go there. I spent my time in French class feeling the urge to go straight to the bucket that was right in front of the teacher's desk. Once French class was over I forced my way into math class. I couldn't bear the thought of making a fool of myself, puking in front of my classmates again. I spent the whole day with the urge to vomit. My professor had to pass me the bucket to regurgitate in a couple of days prior. They all started laughing at me. I ran across the room in tears with my sweater wrapped around my waist. I started seeing their heads in bubbles, laughing at me all at once. Never have I been so embarrassed in my life. My teacher made it worse when he said out loud that I needed get a hold of myself. He said he was sick and tired of dealing with me.

To escape these people, Harmony was the only place that I thought of; it was the place where I was not a burden or problem. Being with the animals I could forget about everything, including the unpleasant things that have been said about me during French class that day. Unlike the students at school, they welcomed me into their circle of friends. They didn't bully me; these guys were content with my presence. They didn't see me as the fat girl who suddenly was shedding weight unknowingly or the stinky girl who wore the same outfit every day. To them I was a human being, a coy girl who seems to have lost herself in a poor and somewhat materialistic small town.

These animals knew me. They understood me just like I understood them. If the world was more like them the thought of fear would be mythical. Waking up every day in fear would no longer be a thing that I slept and woke up into. Being there as often as I was, I made up names for my new friends. Calling them animals was inappropriate to me. I don't see them as animals. Calling them that would be just as ignorant as the things they've said to me at school. The squirrels are good listeners; a good name for them would be the Attenders. Every time I came to see them, they were the first pack I'd see. There were a total of five squirrels. One thing that struck me when it comes to them was that they were always together, all five of them, happy to see me. In a way I was their mother, a mother who has learned how to treat her kids through my beloved mother. I learned what to do and what not to do when it comes to them. They were the ones who enjoyed eating my food the most compared to the others. If I couldn't eat, I was happy to see someone else showing interest in my food.

With the birds there was so many of them. I couldn't even keep count. When they speak I understood them clearly. Under Harmony's roof they made sure that I was taken care of. When I was feeling down, they sang to me beautiful lullabies. The sounds that come out of their beaks were indescribable. They sang songs of the afterlife, how it was a beautiful place to be at, an unimaginable place full of joy and happiness. In the beginning, not knowing what they were capable of, I misunderstood the meaning of their lullabies. It wasn't until the day my soul finally departed from my body that I found out their yodel meant that they knew my time here on Earth was short. They were preparing for what's to come next for me. Through the songs they were letting me know that it was okay to allow myself to let go of what I was holding on to, which was my meaningless life. After finding out about the things that I needed answers to, death was not so bad after all. They were smart birds. They came in different colors—white, blue, bright yellow, red. They were the colors of the rainbow. Some were small, and some were big, and some were just blessed with different shapes. They were the most amazing things I've ever seen. A good name for them was Lucid; they were the beings who knew of my past and future.

Then there were the swans that were as white as pure cotton; they came in threes. They were fast and full of life. The little river that flows miles away from the bridge was their home, a place with refreshing water that only I saw the good in. The swans were the angels who held me together as I came in contact with death. With rocks and vines that surround the edges of the river, the water was good to do everything in. It was the place where I took showers in. That water had something magical in it. In the water I'd see the image of my dead mother sharing laughter with me. She was there with me when I was in the water. Being in the water, I was healed. The idea of being sick was erased in my mind, and at times I'd completely forget about being raped. The bad memories were replaced with new memories and good ones. I saw nothing but the things that I have wanted for myself and what it would be like if I wasn't dead. I'd see the image of myself in a better home with my mother, full with happiness and joy. In the water I saw what could be and what will never be.

It felt like heaven being there. When I did come to this place I never wanted to leave. What I like most about the place was the fact that it became my own little territory—well, not my own. For a short while I was the only one who knew of it, the only one that could understand the language of the beings. I thought I was delusional at some point because I could understand them. The more I go to the place, the more it became normal to me that they spoke like humans. I was the only person who had spent time with these other beings. I was always the only one there. As far as if other humans could understand them too, I wanted to find out. I wanted to know if I was the only one who had this supernatural gift that understood the mind and language of a different species. The thing is I wanted to find out. However, I didn't want anyone else to hold the gift that only I had. Knowing these species the way I did was one thing that made my life somewhat special. I didn't want anyone else to take that away from me. It was amazing to think that I could understand a different kind of species more than I understood my own kind. I had a secret that no one knew about. I had a lot of secrets that no one knew of, like being raped six years ago by a monstrous man, and now this secret place is added to that list. Not that I anticipate anyone would care to know anyway.

Carole was the only person in my life who appeared to care about my health. Other than that I couldn't think of anyone else who would care. My mother would care; however, she was dead. The only place where I see her was in that river, but the thing was, she wasn't real. It was only my imagination running high. For the short time I knew her, she was candidly a good mother. She loved me when she could. While living with her she didn't let anyone mess with me. I remember one of her drug buddies once called me a rotten girl in front of her; she got up and told her to leave her house if that was the way she was going to speak to me. My mom told her, "If you think my daughter is rotten then you also think I am because she's mine." I never saw that lady again since then.

Occasionally I questioned if my mother made it to heaven or not. If she was in heaven how come she let me suffer so much? Why was it that she had to leave me so soon? My mother left me eight long years ago. I didn't even get a chance to make it at her funeral. I doubted that she had a proper burial. We were poor, and the poor people get buried in a six-foot hole with trash or dust thrown at them to cover them up. That's how it is for the poor people who lived in Haiti; a coffin was never affordable. I was the only family she had, and I wasn't there at her funeral. I can only imagine how wrongly they buried her. I wouldn't be surprised if her soul also wanders around just like I. It makes me livid to know how perished our lives were. We were cursed from any goods. I understand clearly now what my mother used to say to me, that bad things happen to good people and good things happen to bad people. I really see it now. Look at what position I am in now. Most young adults at eighteen are preparing themselves for college while I'm preparing myself for the afterlife, a place or thing I am unsure of. I wish I was one of those people who got it all. Looking at them on TV, they look like they have no worries whatsoever, so sure of what they have. They look healthy and beautiful. In my eyes they were immortals. They seem to have so much life ahead of themselves.

My life is already made up for me. There's no way I can change it. My life was destined to be this way, full of heartache and misery. These famous people were rich and notorious because it was meant for them to be like that. People like me don't get special privileges; our privileges involve struggling to find a place to sleep in each night. A few of us orphans don't even get this privilege. Some sleep in the dusty pavement, thinking of what the next day will bring, and some sleep in the wet grass, hoping to close their eyes for a night of rest until the next day. Our privileges didn't involve being rich or having the opportunity to brag about what America, the New World, offers. People like us get raped, abused, and neglected by foster mothers or made fun of by people who can't stand the idea of orphans living in their community. That's us—we have a "happy life."

I always hated it when it was the weekend. I had to coerce myself to be this healthy little girl for people, especially being in the house with Carole. My appearance may have sold me out; nevertheless, I was trying. I isolated myself in my room, pretending to be something that I was far from being. Staying home with a bunch of screaming kids was another thing that I had to deal with. They fight, they fall, and they mess up the house after Carole spends hours cleaning it. During the weekends I prefer to stay in my room rather to infect anyone with my "diseases." That's what Christina says when I stand next to her. She didn't want to be bothered by someone like me. In her moody days, she calls me "contagious" because I had a constant runny nose, watery eyes, and couldn't keep food from staying in my stomach.

The weekends were a time for everyone to go out. Using her own money, Carole takes everyone out on Sundays for a choice of either breakfast or movies. The kids of course usually go with the movies. The movies were the place they go to socialize with friends from their school. Of course I didn't have any, so I would try to sneak my way out of going with them. I refused to let the other kids see me as a loser. Christina knew I was a loser; she has seen me eating lunch alone at school. The movies were a place for them to hang out and chat with their friends, and I didn't have anyone to do that with. I refused to be seen alone by myself while the other kids taunt me about not having any friends. I went once to the movies with them, and never again did I want to go through that experience. The moment they get home, they ask me, "How come you were all alone by yourself at the movies? Don't you have any friends at school?" I never wanted to answer that question. I didn't want to tell them a lie nor did I want to tell something that would allow them to take advantage of me. Since then I tried my best to avoid the movies, the park, or any activities that involved all of us. I was afraid of being left alone with no place to hide. When they go to the movies, Carole let them watch any movie they want to watch as long as it wasn't an X-rated movie. That's what I like most about Carole. She was never afraid to use her own money to take care of someone else's kid. She was continually considerate to everyone's needs. She wanted everyone to socialize with a friend or two, other than the person they live with, and I was ashamed of myself for being friendless.

I was scared of Christina seeing me alone with no friends as always. She's one of the main reasons I spend time eating my lunch in the bathroom, I refuse to give her a reason to think that I am a loser everywhere I go. She had way too much friends. I can admit now that I was a bit jealous of her. The others usually have two or three friends tagging along with them; not her—she had a whole circle of friends from school. Counting, I would say five of them were boys from the soccer team who thought they were too good for some people and some from the cheerleading circle. And the other two were two girls who would do anything to be "cool" like her. She was seen as the most favorable girl at school. Girls wanted to be her, and boys acted like a dog around her everywhere she went. I came to realize that beauty is like power. She had control over each one of them. She snaps her finger for something and she gets it. She's not getting what she wants from her family, so she finds other ways to get it. I felt obligated to have friends because of her even when I didn't see the purpose of having any. I told Carole that I didn't like movie Sundays; she understood that and let me stay home. And plus, she was saving a few bucks by letting me stay home.

Sooner or later I would have to face my fears of them knowing that I have some sort illness that I have no clue of. I'm starving and I'm hearing my stomach eating away at itself. I wanted to eat, but eating evolved into pain that I couldn't bear going through. I vomit everything I eat. I shredded pounds like sweat. To add to my sickness, I started to see blood in my bile. My short life as I know it was fading from my eyes. What could possibly be wrong with me that my body couldn't heal itself like it did when I was with my mother? My nightmares never went away, unless I went to Harmony and slept there. Seeking to close my eyes, I see nothing but flashbacks of horror. It was wrong of me to keep skipping school, considering it was only for five hours that went by real quick. Part of me knew that the reason I was so sick was because of the assailant. My sickness started after that incident. He left me mentally sick on that cold corridor to the point where I became physically sick as time progressed. I prayed to God that he give me a different body to be in. That was impossible. When I couldn't find a way to feel better other than when I was with Harmony, I began to lose it and wanted to see a doctor. I didn't have money. What was the point if they were just going to diagnose me and send me home?

Carole was staying home with me as often as she could, once again coming to my rescue. I can't count how many times this woman have stopped everything for me. She was the only thing I had close to having a mother. She came into my room, waking me up for school, when she notices that there is a spot of dry blood on the pillow, and my breathing is radically shallow. She screamed for my name. "Jasmine, Jasmine, are you okay?" I faintly responded to her that I was okay. If I was afraid of the hospital then that day was the day that I was going after ten years of trying to avoid it. I had no voice left in me. My throat was dry, ached. Furthermore, I was in pain. With my scabby lips, anything I tried to say made it worse. I heard her saying that she was going to call 911. I couldn't stop her. The phone was in the kitchen, and I didn't have the energy to run after her. Before I knew it I was in an ambulance that resembled a broken-down taxi cab. They took me to the hospital and the rest went blurry from there. When I woke up I saw Carole standing next to my hospital bed, sobbing. Trying to sit up, I realized that I was wired in. I couldn't move my arms, my legs; every part of my body felt numb. I was fastened to the bed. I had so many things hooked up to my body it appeared unreal to me. Carole told me that I've been in the hospital for a good three days. She asked me if I was able to talk. I asked her what's wrong with me. She took a while to answer me. I asked if everything was going to be okay, and judging by all the wires and tubes I was hooked into, I already knew the answer. I was never going to live a normal life. I just needed her to tell me everything will be okay. I was a mortal soul lying in a hospital bed, waiting for the doctors to pull the plug on me. After all, I had no money.

Carole held my hand and told me the reason that I have been so sick was because I have been dealing with a chronic disease called HIV, and I never knew of it. I looked at her and told her that she was out of her mind. I said to her, "I'm only seventeen. This is impossible." I didn't know much about the disease, only that you get it from having sex. "I have never had sex with anyone except for . . ." Then I resigned to being mute. I didn't want to continue to explain myself to Carole. My intent was never to have her think that I'm a bad person. I also didn't want her thinking I was sleeping around. I lay in the hospital bed with teardrops, not knowing what's going to happen to me next.

The doctor came into my room and told me that he needed to know how many people I have slept with, not giving me a chance to explain myself. He tells me that I need to give him the name and phone numbers of those I have slept with because I have infected them with HIV also. Listening to the doctor talking like that about me made me feel despicable. I went on to tell him that I have never slept with anyone. He squints his eyes at me, and at that moment, I knew that he didn't believe me. I told him I had no friends, let alone people to have sex with. "Look at me. Do

I look like someone people would sleep with?" Boys run away from me; they think that I have a distinctive smell. I went on to tell him that the only human that has been willing to stay next to me is this woman right here, Carole. She was the only human who didn't mind being around me.

The doctor continued to ask me the same question over again, to see if I would change my response. "You need to tell me the truth. Otherwise, I can't help you or the others who you also gave that disease to." I told him again and again that the thought of boys repulsed me. He said, "I don't understand. Then how did you end up with this disease at such a young age? The only way I can see this happening is you contracting this from your mother during her pregnancy, but the doctor would have already detected that. If you have never had sex like you said then you either got it from your mother or got it from being in contact with the blood of someone who has it. Do you inject drugs into your body, dear?" My mom may have done drugs, but she was not a slut. She hated guys just as much as I did. After my father left her when he found out that she was pregnant with me, she vowed to never let a man come into her life ever again. I have never injected anything into my body. Being with my mother for such a short period, I have gotten the chance to learn what to do and what not to do. Everything the doc was asking me I had no answer to. Now it was up to me to tell him the truth about where I think I may have contracted the disease.

Carole and the doctor sat by my bed, waiting to hear the explanation of how a seventeen-year-old girl not even out of high school is HIV positive. I feel like my nightmares are starting to affect the people close to me. The time has come for me to face the reality of what started all of this. It's just like when that man threw himself on me six years ago. I was scared to tell them what this man took from me. Most importantly I was scared of what Carole would think of me when she hears my reason for what started all of this. I had no choice when it came to keeping my secret a secret. I had fears that my nightmares would haunt me even more if anyone ever found out. That moment, sitting in the hospital bed, was a do-or-die moment. If I didn't tell the doctor and Carole how I may have contracted this disease, I was afraid he wouldn't allow himself to help a girl like me. My life depended on it. My secret could no longer be kept a secret. Fearing what they might think of me, I swallowed my pride and began to tell them of what happened to me that night in 1972. Carole was in shock as I continued to tell her my story. The doctor had a questioning look on his face as he put the tip of his pen in his mouth. He shakes his head back and forth twice before he proceeded to ask me if I knew the guy and his whereabouts. The only thing that I knew about the man was that he lived on the side of the streets five blocks from the previous orphanage I lived at. The streets were his home. Once the incident happened he vanished. Now he lives in my head when I go to bed or doze off at school. He found ways to haunt me anywhere I was, that's what I told the doctor. Of course with Carole around listening to every bit of information I'm feeding to the doctor, she made it clear to the doctor that whatever treatment I was going to get there was no way she or I could pay for it. She appeared speechless with her hands over her head.

With shallow breaths one after the other, she managed to say, "How come you never told anyone about this? The minute he did this act on you, you should have gone to your foster mom and told her about this. You should have reported this to the police, Jasmine, and now it's too late!" Carole walks around the room like a crazy person panicking about what I've just told her. I couldn't tell anyone, and even if I did, my ex-foster mother would have called me a liar. She never cared about what I and the other kids had to say. If I went to the police and explained to them how I became a victim, they would have turned their backs on me, making me feel less important than I was. They would think my case was too little of a case to waste their time on. Around here people got away with anything, even murder. Once you're dead, you become forgotten, and once you've become a victim of rape, you become voiceless. There's no such thing as justice for the poor or the orphans. For people like me, it was a matter of being heard, a matter of finding the voice that we once had. Sitting in that hospital bed was when my life completely turned upside down. The thing they spoke so little of at school had somehow found its way to me. Given my explanation, Dr. Jean showed less interest in me as he chose to tell me the symptoms of my disease.

"Experiencing the high fever, the sore throat, the vomiting, the weight loss were all signs of HIV." How was I sixteen, an orphan, and HIV positive? Why were all the wrong things happening to me? What else could happen next? I had everything that could possibly be wrong happening to me. I couldn't be hurt anymore. Anything that needed to be done was done. My curse couldn't be broken; the spell that was put upon my mother found its way to her only offspring.

Tears of sadness have overshadowed my hospital room. Carole was crying, and I was crying, contemplating how short my life will be with this disease that had no end to it. Just when I thought I was going to feel better one day. Just when I thought Carole's aid will end it. It seems like it was just the beginning of the worse to come for I, Jasmine Pierce. There was nothing unique about that name. It was nothing, but a curse.

"Do you mind stepping out of the room for a few minutes? I need to talk to Jasmine alone, please," the doctor says. What else could he possibly tell me that I didn't know already? I have heard everything that he had to say already. What could have been worse than being diagnosed with HIV? Please, God, tell me that I'm dreaming. Tell me that I will wake up and find out that this is only just a dream. That's all I thought about as the doctor walked Carole out of the door.

The doctor approached me and said, "I am just going to tell you this straight up. This is a lot to deal with, especially being seventeen and all. That's a lot to take in. Now I know you don't have money for the procedures that's needed to be done, that's what's going to hurt you the most. If I sit here and tell you that I'm going to try my best to keep you alive for longer than expected, I would be lying to you. Trying my best requires money. You have none of that! I have more bad news. Since we discovered this too late, you're no longer in the virus stage. Since you weren't getting medications, the disease has spread faster to your immune system than anticipated."

He went on to explain what the disease was doing to my body. HIV infects cells in the immune system and the central nervous system. One of the main types of cells that HIV infects is the T helper lymphocyte. These cells play a crucial role in the immune system by coordinating the actions of other immune system cells. A large reduction in the number of T helper cells seriously weakens the immune system. Over time, HIV infection leads to a severe reduction in the number of T helper cells available to help fight disease. HIV infection can generally be broken down into four distinct stages: primary infection, clinically asymptomatic stage, symptomatic HIV infection, and progression from HIV to AIDS.

"At this point right now you're are at the symptomatic stage." He tells me that any flu symptoms or sickness can trigger the infection for the worse. "I don't really know how long it's been since you've been with it, but I can tell you the stages are moving fast." He tries to explain clearly to me what is happening right now with the symptomatic stage. He tells me that my immune system is being severely damaged by this stage. The lymph nodes and tissues have been damaged; HIV infections mutate and become more pathogenic—in other words, stronger and more varied, leading to more T helper cell destruction. Your body fails to keep up with replacing the T helper cells that are lost. As your immune system fails, the symptoms develop. Typically, many of the symptoms are mild, but as the immune system deteriorates, the symptoms worsen. "May God be with you, child," he says as he ended his lecture of what was happening to my body. I was getting nauseated just listening to him explain what was happening. My head was spinning in every direction. I needed to be away from it all. I need to be with Harmony. I felt restless.

When I thought things was going to change, things just changed for the worst. I thought hospitals were supposed to make people feel better, not make the sick feel helpless. I hated the place and I no longer wanted to be a part of it. "I'm trying the best I can, but judging from data you have seven months to live. With proper care and you taking some of the medications that you can afford, I'm sure you can beat the odds and live longer than that, but if you're not getting any treatments, seven months is all you'll have." That's what the doctor told me, that I was going to die soon and money stood in the way of me living longer. The doctor's greed was insulting to me. The only thing that was standing in the way of my health was money.

He called Carole back into the room and gave her a list of medications for her to pick up for me at the pharmacy. I knew for a fact there's no way I had enough funds for these medications. The donations were coming to the house less and less. At some point Carole had to use her own money to feed the fourteen of us, including herself. Imagine if now she has to deal with buying extra things. These extra things weren't just things. They were things that I needed in order to stay alive, just like the other kids needed their food to keep them going, and they were equally important. Whatever money we had left was not going to be enough for these expensive medications. We barely had enough for food. Picture my monthly refilled medications being on the list, HIV medications. The doctor gave me seven months to live. Mentally I was already dead the moment I held my mother and watched her die in front of me, and then I died again when I was taken to the hospital and woke up to find myself all wired up with tubes and IVs attached to my body. I was a living zombie waiting to turn into dust. When the pity money completely stops, that would determine the rest of my being here on Earth. When I turn eighteen, the little checks will stop coming. What will happen to me then? I'm seventeen going on eighteen; that is the age every aid stops. That's the age they kick me out, to find my way alone. With seven months left according to the doctor, I knew life was short for me. It wasn't like regular people living their lives, not knowing when death will hit. In about seven months death will hit me, and the people who surrounded me were aware of it. They knew to prepare themselves for what's ahead. By them, I meant

Carole. She was the only person who looked after me when it comes to my illness. I can't help but wonder that it was faith that brought us together in my days of hopelessness. She struggled with the news more than I did. In the time I needed someone, she was there for me acting like the mother I lost years ago. She was not ready to let me go, and I was not ready to lose the thing I had closest to a mother. When I was younger I wanted to have a family of my own so that I could correct the mistakes that my mother made or the mistake that I have made. Knowing that my time was near, all was crushed by one heartless man. If only he could see how wounded he left me. He should have ended my life on that dark alley once he was done. The suffering he caused me can never be erased. The doctor rushed to discharge me from the hospital. I wasn't stable to go home. With no health insurance and no money, I was more than ready to go home according to their system. I was sent home with a list of medications that I couldn't afford. He sent me home to get ready for death. With a condescending doctor dealing with my case, a second chance at life or making me a charity case was not on his mind when he knew that I was poor. When Carole and I left the hospital he didn't flinch or look back. Right after we put our foot outside his office, he shut the door on us. He couldn't wait to watch us impecunious people leave his territory. The more time we spent in his office, the more to him it appears we were taking his rich clients away from him. He never believed me when I told him that I have never slept with anyone. He didn't have to say it. His facial expression was enough. He took my story very loosely when he asked me, "Are you sure you didn't have consensual sex with him? Kids like you have been known for these kinds of exposure, having sex with different men for money." Other kids may have done what he says, but I wasn't that kind. It didn't matter if I explained myself to him or not. To him I was an orphan who had little supervision. Therefore, I was on the street sleeping with men I didn't know. He believed whatever he wanted to believe. Telling him what happened to me was nothing but a change of character in my part. He had Carole thinking that I was an unsupervised harlot who has caught a disease from one of these fictional men he spoke of.

Paranoid about the new twist in my life, I was a bit happy to be back in the orphanage after days of being tied up in the hospital like a lab rat for nothing, only to be told that I had seven months to live, and due to my lack of funds there was nothing they could do to help increase my life expectancy. When the other kids saw me coming, they all came to say hi to me, which was very unusual. They didn't get too close to me, but they all got close enough to welcome me back to the orphanage. I looked at them and smiled. I smiled back at them, not because I knew Carole must have spoken to them about my disease while I was in the hospital, but because they were trying to be nice to the poor HIV-infected orphan girl. It was forced, I could tell. To me it was okay. It wasn't very often that Carole could get these kids to not be in conflict with me. I took what I could get from them. They got the words to come out of their mouths, and for that it was a triumph and a smiling moment for me. They acted as if they didn't know what was wrong with me but still kept their distance from me. They sympathized with my situation, but the idea of coming near me disgusted them even more now that they know I'm dealing with this chronic disease.

Carole brought me straight to my room. Upon my arrival to the house, already I was feeling claustrophobic and nauseated. I was feeling close to death already. I took my medicine, and within a few hours I was throwing up. I wasn't strong enough to deal with this. The effect of the medicines took a toll for the worst. My body had a strong reaction to the medicines. I couldn't keep anything down. My body was too small to handle such strong drugs. My fever was higher than ever. I couldn't stop sweating even with the amount of cold towels Carole had laying on my body. My pupils were dilating; even I was getting scared of them. Little by little I was starting to look like the girl from the American movie *The Exorcism of Emily Rose*—skinny, pale, and bruised up. As a dark-skinned girl, my skin became colorless; my once-flawless dark skin became grayer. I was pretty sure the change of my skin color came from the side effects of the drugs. My skin became very sensitive; a wrong rub from the overused sheets we had at the orphanage would leave a mark on my body. I had blisters that were growing inside my lips and in my private parts. The more I hid myself from the public, the more my eyes became open to the possibility of just ending my life. The medication was supposed to make me feel better, filter my immune system, but no one would believe me if I told them that they're doing the opposite. For the next two months I felt worse, way even before I started taking them. I couldn't sleep, I couldn't eat, and I missed my mother much more than usual. I stayed home every day, hiding in my room while I watched everyone through the window, leaving the house for different outings—school and getting picked up by their friends to go out. I was comfortless, empty, and alone in a little bathroom-sized secluded area where I isolated myself from the public. Even being seen at the house by the other kids became scary to me. Friendless, I got scared more and more every day. The place where I felt it was acceptable to be seen by the public, I couldn't go, in my condition, Harmony seems miles and miles away. Carole told me that because of the appearance of my body I was going to be excused from school until my body recovers. Now I'm not stupid. The real reason as to why I couldn't go was because my disease can't be contained. She was afraid that I would pass it on to those close to me. At the orphanage I was only allowed in my room and in my room only. Carole had to bring things to me. I couldn't go get anything by myself. When she was out, I was to wait for her if I needed anything. In the house, my plate, my spoon, and my chair were marked. No one was to use anything I used. As for taking showers, I couldn't take a shower at the house or defecate in the house. The only time I was allowed to leave the orphanage if Carole was not around was if I needed to defecate. I was to leave the house, walk twelve minutes away from the orphanage, and get my business done on a stranded bush that contains my defecations for months. I was to come back right after. There were times when I ran out of spots to do my business in. As bad as it sounds, I couldn't complain. At least I still had a place to sleep in at the orphanage. Carole would walk a mile away with a bucket marked with the letter *J*, filled with water for my bath. Since she found out that I was positive, she stopped giving me showers. While she stands a distance away from me, she guides me with the showers. I was sad she couldn't take care of me the way she used to, but it was for the best that she protects herself from any bodily fluid of mine. In order to remain at the house I had to obey the rules when it comes to my case. Carole was doing me a favor by not telling the headmaster of the orphanage about my situation. Carole's job was on the line for me. Now I have met the owner of the orphanage. He's nothing but a money-hungry guy. I have heard rumors that not all the charity money makes it to the house, which was part of the reason why Carole sometimes finds herself using her money to feed us. Nelson was his name. He came once a month to check on the house and also to give Carole some of the leftover charity money appointed to us. There were thirteen of us in the house. Some months he comes in saying, "Four hundred dollars is what we received in charity money this month. Make it last." He was a sixty-year-old hunchback man who was very cautious when it comes to money. When he comes in he'd even asked Carole if there was any money left from last month.

Nelson doesn't allow sick kids in his orphanage 'cause he thinks sick kids spend his money. With sick kids, it means spending money on them to take them to the hospital, and he wanted no part of that. Ryan was sick once from having the chicken pox. It was said one thousand dollars was needed to treat him. If not, he was going to die. With hesitations and after contemplating it, it took him a couple of days until he finally gave his consent that he was going to pay for the treatment. If he was not using the orphanage's charity money, Carole said he could have gotten the treatment within hours, but because of the cheap kind of man Nelson was, it took him many days until he could let the greed of money out of his system. Now Ryan got his treatment and was able to come back to the orphanage looking like a new kid. However, what about me? Nelson would not risk spending hundreds of thousands of dollars on me. We didn't really see eye to eye that much. When he was around I hid myself from him, especially when the blisters were growing around my mouth. Mr. Nelson, being the crude man that he was, would have sent me packing instantly had he known I was positive, and the school would expel me if they ever find out that one of their very own students was dealing with the thing they spoke least about, the thing teachers were scared to talk about. I could infect an overpopulated school of three thousand or a classroom of thirty-six, according to the school system.

With Carole's job being on the line, she tried her best to keep me hiding from him for months. If Nelson finds out about my rare case, he'll kick me out for my death, not caring about the fact that I had no one outside the orphanage. Parentless and alone, I would find myself doing the same thing I used to do when I lived at the previous orphanages, begging on the streets for survival. He didn't care. He was a cold man who would do anything to keep people from getting close to his money. Hours away from the orphanage there was a clinic for the severely ill called "Lhopitale pour la Maladie." It was the hospital where they made the impossible possible. They could treat the mentally ill, the cancerous, and the HIV positives. There was where all the treatments were done for rare diseases that couldn't be treated at the regular hospital, the regular hospital where doctors like Jean makes it a big deal to be seen. Lhopitale pour la Maladie was the place where the survival rate for HIV tripled. If you've gone through that hospital, the chances of beating the odds were very high. I've heard artists and movie stars have gone through that place and come out of it disease free. These people are living among us, bragging about beating the odds. That hospital had flaws. It wasn't for people like me, outsiders. We could only hear talks about it. It made us feel like we were nobody, knowing that we could never afford to get treatment there. It was nothing but a tease. People say it was impeccable, but to me and others like me who were suffering, it was impeachable. It was meant for the Haitian chivalries, not for the Haitian unfortunates.

For entertainment I watched the lives of the negatives through a hole in my room, experiencing what it means to live a happy and healthy life. In them I saw what I have always wanted my whole life. I have to admit watching them through the hole encouraged my imagination. Sitting in that little room for two months straight, I had a lot of time to ask what if? I did it so much that some of my imaginings became believable to me.

I missed being with Harmony, hanging out with my true friends. These were the kinds of things that helped me forget about my never-ending sickness. Whenever I was with Harmony, the idea of being severely ill never crossed my mind. My mind was occupied by the things that valued my existence. I couldn't keep anything down; my bowel movements were coming out of my rear end every time I sneezed. I no longer had control over it. I couldn't grunt or sneeze. If I did, it was a different story down there. Watching the other kids come in and out of the house made me realize I've never been so alone and so discouraged. They see me, and they make no attempt to see how my life was passing me by. I watch them from the corners of my room, living their lives as if I don't exist to them. My room was my everything—my kitchen, my place to sleep, sometimes even my bathroom when I couldn't hold it in for too long, the place where I wash my clothes and hang them up to dry. Slowly it was becoming a morgue too. There I was shedding pounds. I deteriorate in front of my own eyes, waiting for death to finally strike.

Then finally, a day came when I stopped feeling sorry for myself. I gathered myself together—I bathed myself, combed my hair, and wore something clean. While the other kids and Carole were away, I cleaned the house wearing safety precautions. I kept in mind what the doctor told me: "Stay away from things that could cut you." If anyone came in contact with my blood, there was a possibility of them catching what I have. Since I've been sick, Carole had been the one taking care of me since I left the hospital. She hasn't had time to clean the house. The house was filthy. Passing by the kitchen area, there were spiderwebs blocking the entrance, dirty clothes everywhere, and the bathroom started growing mold. The kitchen was filled with dirty dishes and mice scraping the unwashed dishes. She has been giving to me, and now it was time that I gave back to her. If I couldn't pay her by offering her money then cleaning the house was the least bit I could do. She has been working another job since she learned that the charity money wasn't coming in as often as it used to. She didn't have a family of her own. To her we were not orphans. We were her kids, and she was willing to do anything for us until someone came for us. No one was coming for us. It was a while since anyone new stepped into the orphanage. Some of us had hopes though that someone would come in and take us away from this place. There was nothing wrong with the orphanage; it was overcrowded with no room left to breathe. If it wasn't for Carole, we'd have vanished from the place one by one a long time ago. Carole was what kept the orphanage standing. The paint was peeling off of its interior and its exterior walls; its foundations were decomposing. One strong wind was enough to bring it down. I cleaned the house with the bit of energy that I had in me. She was happy; the smile on her face couldn't be bought. She hugged me. It was the first time in a while she's allowed herself to get this close to me.

She's been with me ever since my arrival here at the orphanage. I was okay. I was feeling better. I shook myself off and told her I was in good shape. I told her that the medicines were working. With the blisters off my body, she took a good look at me and said, "You seem fine. Maybe the medicines are finally working." I told her she could work more if she wanted to. I got tired of seeing her doing my mother's job, taking care of me every second of every minute. She barely had time for the other twelve kids plus herself. She was determined to stick by my side. Convincing her that I was okay to be on my own for now was impossible.

"You look better, but you're not okay."

"I feel fine."

"You can work extra shift now like you've been talking about."

"I'm doing extra shift because I choose to. Never think it's because of you. My job here is to take care of you guys. Jasmine, I want you to know I'm doing everything in my power to make sure you guys are taken care of."

"I can help too. Did you see how I cleaned the house?

"I see that and I couldn't be any happier. The only thing I need you to do when you're here is to rest. By you doing that, you're helping me, okay?"

At night she made home medicines with hopes that I can come out of this. She reads Bible verses to me. A particular verse she reads before bedtime was Solomon chapters 1–2. "By night on my bed I sought him whom my soul loveth: I sought him, but I found him not. I will rise now, and go about the city in the streets, and in the broad ways I will seek him whom my soul loveth: I sought him, but I found him not." Those were her favorite verses. Every night before bedtime she prays and reads them to me. Those verses were becoming my favorite verses from hearing her reading them as often as she did. Another ritual she does before bedtime was massaging my body with this weird scented oil. The first night I came back from the hospital, I refused to put that oil on my body. The scent of it made me nauseated. The scent of it was very unusual. It's smelled like seven-day-old urine with a mixture of Ryan's dirty socks. She knew every medical trick to reduce a fever. Most often her remedies worked on me. The first time she tried to apply that oil on me, I refused it. She was okay with me refusing her oil the first time around. When I woke up the following morning she came into my room and asked me how I felt. Surprisingly and honestly, I felt like I have been reborn. My body was rejuvenated, fresh, and stress free. For the first time since I have been sick, I have never felt this great. In fact I can never remember when, during my lifetime, I had ever felt this great. She told me she had massaged my body with the oil while I was asleep. It's times like this I wish she was my mother, the sober one. She acted like my mother. To her I was not an orphan. She saw me as her daughter, a seventeen-year-old daughter who was running out of time. For a short while I felt great. Her remedies worked but it never lasted.

"Will you be okay to stay home by yourself today?"

"Yeah, I'll be fine, don't worry about me. I'll stay in my room just like you asked."

"All right, I'll see later tonight. There's some white rice in your room in case you're hungry."

"Thanks. When will I be okay to go back to school, Carole?"

"Whenever you feel ready, you let me know, and I'll drive you there myself," she said to me.

I knew what she meant when she said whenever I was ready. She meant whenever I was ready to hide my disease from the school. If I was good enough to hide it from Mr. Nelson then I could hide it from the school as long as students stay out of my way. The school couldn't find out. Although I knew my expiration date, I couldn't make that be a reason to stay away from school. Ultimately, I was focused on finishing my high school year. My mother was a high school dropout, and her goal was to see me graduate high school and college. If going to college was not in my future, I was determined to make her happy by finishing my high school education one way or the other. My goal was to make her proud wherever she was, hell or heaven.

Feeling vacant and drained, I wander around the house, bored out of my mind, friendless and hoping that one day I could pick up that phone that's staring at me to call a friend, someone I can actually talk to about my life. Time goes by fast when all you have to think about is how short your life is, especially when you know your expiration date. Knowing that I have less than five months to live, I should be putting checks on the one hundred things to do before death list, but none were being checked. In Haiti there's no such thing. After watching *The Bucket List*, it was fair to have a list. Or at least accomplish one of those things on my list. I quickly started to make my very own list after watching that movie. It was a very inspiring movie. Number one off the top of the list was to see how my father looked. I wanted to know if I had his lips, his eyes, or his nose. I wanted to meet the man who left my mother to raise a child all alone. The list was one hundred things of impossible things I would never get to accomplish. I never thought that I was going to die at the age of eighteen. It's still a shocker to me. I was so sure that as the year ended I was going to heal from all of this. I always thought that I had to retire from a career first or I had to be sixty-five years old or that I had to be old enough to collect my insurance policy money. My mother once told me that I was going to grow up away from this hateful place to make something of myself. All of the above did not apply to me. I was going to die alone, young, and poor. I was going to die without accomplishing anything for my life or getting the chance to do the number one thing I wanted to do on my list. I felt restricted entirely. My mother has been gone for years, and there wasn't a day that went by when I didn't hold myself accountable for her death. I could have saved her had I gone outside early enough to call out for help. Every now and then I wonder how she would react if she knew that her only daughter was dead. Number two on my list was to see my mother one last time again. Guess that will never happen. Only in the afterlife, if there is such a thing, something that people spoke very highly of. I haven't seen anything out of the ordinary; it's been two hours since I took my last breath. Christina was the first one to come back from school since Carole started working five days a week at the farm. She has not had the time to pick anyone up from school as much. Even then Christina finds time to make it back to the orphanage on time; she's worried about anyone following her to the orphanage, her friends in particular, friends who didn't know she lived in an orphanage. She always gets out of the last class early if Carole wasn't picking her up, which gave her time to walk home first. One day she came home around noontime. This was rare to me. She wasn't the type of girl who skipped school, and she had no reason to. Something must have gone wrong at school that day. I wanted to make an attempt to ask her if everything was okay, but I was scared. I was scared of the answer I might get from her. Every time I tried talking to her, it was always a battle between her and I. Squeezing a conversation out of her was impossible. I made an attempt a few weeks before dying. Her exact words were "Screw you." What is it that I have done to her that made her hate me so much, considering how I have not said anything dreadful about her? At no time has she given me the chance to get to know her, nor has she taken the chance to get to know me as a person, but rather, she judges me based on my outer appearance. She has a vendetta against me. As far as what it was, I was clueless. I lived in the house for two years along with thirteen other people, and out of that thirteen, only one of them accepted me into the orphanage. I understand at times I can be very shy and didn't like to let people get too close to me. The closer they get to me, the more they'd find a way to hurt me. I avoided that as often as the opportunity presented itself. I did appear doleful according to my professors, but it didn't mean that I didn't want friends or people to talk to. I was optimistic the first day I spent with Carole, and seeing so many kids living under one little roof, I was very optimistic about making new friends here in a new town. I thought I was going to start my orphanage life fresh all over again. Starting over was my motive. I was open to the idea of replacing my bad memories with good ones. I was wrong. People see me, and they find a good laugh out of me. It was not because I was popular at school. As far I could remember the toilet seats were more popular than I was. Being popular, making friends was something that I could fantasize about, and that was as popular as I would get.

While walking around the house, I stumbled upon Christina's schoolbag. I stopped and said to her, "What have I done to you to make you hate me so much?"

She replied back while staring at me from head to toe with this I'm-better-than-you look. "No one talked to you, Jasmine. Look at you and look at me. What do you see?"

"Christina, I didn't choose to look this way. I wish you could switch places with me so you can see and feel how you make me feel. You think you're better than everyone here, don't you?"

"I am! Especially when it comes to you. If only you could hear the things people say about you at school."

"Oh I know. You don't have to tell me. Why are you home this early anyway?"

"Hey, you want to know a secret? I'm working on finding my mother."

"Really? I'm so happy for you." I had so many questions to ask her but held them in because for the first time in my life I had someone sitting next to me, having a normal conversation with me. I told her, "I have no doubt in my mind that you will find her."

"Do you want to come in my room?"

Had she forgotten that I was positive? Why was she not avoiding my disease? How was this possible? She's talking to me. I didn't go to school. I have no idea what could have happened to Christina that switched her from being the beast of the house to this good girl that I'm meeting for the first time. I hadn't come across this girl before. Maybe someone hit her in the head, or maybe Daphne from French class had finally reached her soft side. Whatever or whoever it was, they were now known as my god or goddesses. I had never been inside her room before; I've only peeked at it from outside, catching a little glimpse of her bed, which she shared with Adeline and Emma. Amazed by how the room was kept well maintained, I questioned myself if she was the favorite one at the house. After all, Mr. Nelson did pay more attention to her when he comes for his monthly visits. Her room looks better than the rest of the orphanage. Looking at the orphanage from the outside, one would never guess there was a room in there that looked the way her room did. It was decent for someone who was taken care of by charity money. Her room was bratty just like she was. Her room was pink and embedded with posters of dolls. She was a bit too old to for the doll phase. I'm not really a pink fan, even if I like the pink décor. Everything that was in her room was pink. She even had pink carpet to go with the rest of the room. A couple months ago there was no carpet. And who would have thought a tough girl like Christina would have pink as her favorite color and still play with dolls? It seems like while I was hiding in my room, Nelson had been taking real good care of Christina, better than any of the other kids. She had new clothes every month while the others wore the same wrinkly, worn-out T-shirt and ripped-up jeans three times a week. It was made very clear who the favorite was at the orphanage. She took a shirt that was on her bed and held it near my face, saying, "This shirt can do you some good. Try it on. I've only worn it once." As I tried to put the shirt on, I sneezed into the shirt. I got scared of what she would do. I stood in silence, waiting to hear her reaction. She pulled the shirt down my head, fixing it on me. She looked at me and said, "There, you're pretty already. You can wear this to school tomorrow." I have no idea who this stranger was. She must have wanted something from me. I couldn't give her anything. I have nothing. Some angel must have taken over her body, was the only thing I could think of. This was not the Christina I met almost two years ago. Something was going on and I needed to find out what. She was too nice. The things that I discovered she had in her room, there was no way she could afford them; and yes, Nelson did offer her more attention than any of us, but he loved his money way too much to be spending it on expensive clothes on her. I could understand the new carpet and the dolled-up wall but not a closetful of unworn dresses, jeans, and shoes. She was just a foster kid, not the daughter of a queen. Daphney was the rich girl in school, yet Christina played the role best—mean, arrogant, and egocentric. In the public eye she was all wrapped up in herself. I wanted to get to the bottom of this. Later that same week I told Carole that I was ready to go back to school. The medicines were kicking into my system. I felt somewhat "better." I went to school wearing Christina's shirt, feeling sick and out of my element. The school looked different, or maybe it was I that looked different. That day I was not wearing the oversized ripped jacket or the overworn black jeans that were turning gray. I was wearing a nice long-sleeved brown shirt and blue jeans owned by Christina, my orphanmate. Her clothes fit my 109-pound frame perfectly. I went from 230 pounds of pure fat to

180. As I got more and more sick, my weight dropped down to an exasperating 109 pounds of hanging skin that seems to remain perfectly hidden under Christina's long-sleeved shirt. I looked at myself in the mirror and asked myself what was happening to me. I was disappearing before my own eyes. Like always, people were staring at me grossly while walking along the corridor of Judem Valley High. The school looked different, but the people sure did not change from the couple of months that I had been away for my illness. I was clean, fresh, and wearing brand-new clothes. No one noticed though. The students still treated me the same. The shoving against the locker, the pencil flicking, and calling me "that girl" still remained the same. I hated the school. I didn't hate the school because I was learning something or at least I was trying to. I hated it because of the students it was teaching. I wanted to learn something at school, but the students wouldn't allow it, just like the school wouldn't allow it if they found out I was HIV positive. It didn't matter what I did to prove to them I deserved a chance. Changing my clothes, my outlook, or having a new hairdo, they still managed to look down on me. My disguise didn't mean anything to them. In fact, it sold me very quickly. Every day was just a new day at Judem Valley High. Nothing ever changes, and it remained that way.

With no support, I was the target for hazing and bullying, and inside my head I wanted to scream to put an end to it all. I dealt with a deadly disease at home, and at school I dealt with persecutions from my very own colleagues. Having lunch in the bathroom was becoming too familiar to me. Daphne, who was my classmate, started bringing lunch to school. Britney, the rich girl, doesn't bring lunch to school. Instead she has her chauffeur pick her up during recess to go eat at the fancy restaurant a block away from the school. Daphne brags about being this fortunate. According to her fellow classmates, she was too good for school lunch or food that weren't freshly served to her. I guess not anymore! Often she was licking her fingers from the same old butter sandwiches. I felt sorry for her, sorry enough to think about offering her some of my rice and beans. Little by little I saw more of me in her. Her parents must have been really broke for her to be in this situation when not so long ago she was the social butterfly of Judem Ville. She was no longer rocking the designer outfits made from America. Not knowing that the bathroom was my cafeteria, at times sitting on the toilet I would hear her crying and mumbling things to herself. I could never get close enough to know why her life was falling apart so fast. Later that day in math class she was awfully nice to me. I only could remember one time since my arrival at Judem Valley High that she was this nice to me, and it was when I was in the bathroom throwing up bile. She took a look back and asked me if I was all right. November 3 marked the second day that she was nice to me, and that was six months after the bathroom incident. This was a holiday that needed to be marked on my calendar. The boy that sat beside me, John Sansoux, decided throwing paper balls at me was the way to make class time more entertaining. After he threw the third paper ball at me, Daphne got up and said to him, "Hey! Aren't you a little too old to be throwing paper balls at Jasmine? You always pick her to poke fun of. Why don't you rotate and pick on someone your own size? Matter of fact, why don't you pick on me, coward? I dare you!" Within a matter of seconds John turned around and put his head down. The professor asked Daphne to step out of class for a few minutes. In reply, she told him as well, "Really, Professor? Did you not see what John was just doing to her? You should be telling him to cool off, not me." The whole class got silent, and I, out of embarrassment, I ran out of the class. I was not crying. I was happy that finally someone had stood up in front of a class of thirty-six and defended me; and most important of all, Daphne, the girl who was always calling me names, knew who I was. She knew my name, and she stood up for me in front of my hated peers. I don't know if I was in denial again. Daphne's outlook on certain things changed. Maybe there was a catch to this, I told myself. First, Christina, the girl whom I shared a home with, who never said anything to me, had shared something personal with me along with a brand-new outfit that was wearable to school. Then came Daphne, who stood up for me in class in front of so many. With her reputation on the line, she defended me during my time of weakness. Yes, her reputation was somewhat ruined. Held back after her little speech, it was enough to have him bow his head on the wooden desk. After these two memorable moments, as my world starts to be recognizable, my body failed to keep me from achieving my goals.

As my life descends, the world of my enemies starts to unfold. I commenced to see their personal self, which they've tried to hide from the rest of the population. It was a surprise to me to see the people I hated and envied were becoming my friends secretly, or at least I thought. Their generosities were the start of friendships. They both hated each other too. It's funny to see how things work. If I were alive right now, I'd bravely tell each one of them how they truly made me feel throughout my life. My soul wanders in the city of Judem Ville. I see the cruelty that is being done to kids like me. It was when I died that I saw that I was not the only kid who was suffering from the hands of my own kind strictly because our pockets told a different story. Anyway, let's continue with the story.

The medicines were kicking in as predicted by Dr. Jean. I was vomiting less, although I never stopped shedding pounds. Since my diagnosis, I went from a staggering 109 to a shocking 90 pounds. Carole did try her best to help me keep the weight on. Life is nothing but humorous. It also poked fun at itself. I was never a sexual person, but somehow I found myself dying from a killer disease, a disease that I had very limited resources for. This disease didn't care who its target was, and worst of all it was incurable; I feel bad for the next poor girl who will take my place. How could I, Jasmine Pierce, eighteen years old, be dead from it? I did answer my question. It didn't care about who its victim was. That's what I gathered since I had no parents to teach me how to avoid being a victim of a serial killer. My mom died; this was inevitable.

My only resource was Carole, who herself was overworked, tired, and was coercing herself to do what needed to be done for us at the orphanage. No one knew how hurt I was from being parentless. They created you, but yet in the end they forget about your existence, my father especially, a coward whom I've dreamt of meeting one day. I should hate him for leaving my mother to raise his kid by herself. I should despise him for being in this position, but no. Watching kids at the bus stop with their fathers only brought my attention to feel what they feel. I want to hate him, but my heart wouldn't let me. I've never met the man, yet I've built a life inside my head where he and I lived blithely in a world full of joyful imaginations, where everything impossible becomes promising. Any free time I'd get inside my head from the haunted man, I strive to fill it with an imaginary father.

Every now and then I see my mother's drug-addict friend Annabel in the streets, doing what she loved most in the world, the woman who supposedly was my mom's best friend, the one that ran away as fast as she could after seeing my mom lying dead in my arms with white cream coming out of her mouth. And to think when I was with my mother I saw her as the next closest someone I had to an aunt. My mother didn't have a sister that I knew of, but she always told me to call Annabel by "Auntie Annabel," and I did. I have to admit she did make me laugh when I was down. When my mother couldn't cook for me, she'd come over and made sure I was taken care of. She lent my mother money when she needed money. In a way she was my mother's emergency income.

I never heard from her after the death of my mother. Every now and then I find myself worrying about her safety. Looking down below, I don't think she remembers her godchild, the godchild she shared many laughters with eighteen years ago. In the corner of the streets she opens her legs for men, strangers, just for a quick high. She didn't change much; she still remains in the same area where my mother lived before she died. Blocks away from where I was taken over by orphanage authorities, she was now working in the back of strange men's wagons. All this time I've been gone, she does not seem to have changed one bit. Well, she has changed a little. Instead of working the clothing factory she was doing something else for work to feed her habits. Change was not something people were familiar with around here. Moving forward with life was the enemy to this population.

To buy her crack now she sells her body to the cheapest bidder. Her appearance is nothing like I knew it from when I was nine. She used to have this milky chocolate skin, hair all permed up, and was somewhat healthy looking. I can't even grasp the idea in my head that this woman who's on the streets at night, wearing fishnet tights, is my godmother, the woman who helped deliver me in the kitchen, the woman who cut my umbilical cord and thought throwing my umbilical cord outside my mother's house in the bush was going to bring my mother and I nothing but good luck. She was now a stronger addict than before. My mother told me many great stories about Annabel. I forever kept them with me as a reminder that I too had people that once loved me. She has gotten deeper into her drugs now. I don't seem to matter much anymore. Her skin looks discolored and gray, and she was real skinny, just like me before I fell into a coma and died. I was invisible, and still I was embarrassed that this was someone who was close to my dearest mother. I don't think she knows or thinks about the godchild she lost ten years ago; getting her drugs was her priority, and I saw that in her eyes. She was lost and needed to be found. She doesn't seem to let just anything get in the way of getting her substances. At least I know when I was sick and needed someone to be there for me, I had Carole. She stood by me through thick and thin. In the orphanage she was my mother and my friend, and that's exactly the kind of person Annabel needs to be found by.

Four months following my diagnosis there were times when I felt sick, sick to the point where I couldn't hold myself together, and then there were times when I felt healed. With Carole doing her Haitian home remedies for me and on top of taking my prescribed medications I felt like I was the healthiest kid on Earth. Just like that too, there were times I felt one step closer to death.

Carole never gave up on me. At some point I felt like her home remedies were even better than the prescribed medications.

More and more Christina started to let me into her "personal life," or was it that she was using her sob stories to control me? I did have a weakness for the sadness. As manipulative as she was, part of me didn't believe, and I had doubts about her stories. No longer did I fear talking to her. Knowing that I was expected to live up to three more months, I allowed her to have pity on me. Again she was best at taking advantage of the weak, and I was at my weakest point the moment I entered the orphanage. I was an easy target for her. Of course there were some things I had to agree with before she could make me an official "friend." Knowing that I had no friends I had agreed to her requirements. After all she was a "tough" girl who liked pink. Her shell may have acted tough, and I may have abided by her toughness. There was only one girl who didn't buy her tough attitude. Daphne. Christina may have stolen the spotlight from her at school, but she wasn't going to be just another girl for her to control.

Her friendship rules were I had to agree to never sit on the chairs that she sits on at the orphanage and agree to never use the dinnerware where she eats her dinner or breakfast on. Again, she also wrote her name on them too. She made me swear to never tell anyone at school that we shared the same house. If I could agree to those things then she'd be my friend, but only at home. All of these things, I was already doing them. Everything I could use was marked with my name on them. I was being reassured, I supposed. Those were the things that energized her, reminding me of the things that I already knew of unfortunately. Having control and say over me reassured her that I was just bait to her. At the time I was naïve and in need of a human friend. I shook my head and told her, "Yes, I'll do anything you say." I agreed to her wishes and moved on with her next task. The kids in the house didn't pay much attention to what has been going on with me. They knew my time was very limited. I would have loved to become part of their circle. They were scared of me, afraid that I would get them sick, but I couldn't blame them for watching out for themselves. They kept their distance from me at the orphanage. They feared being too close to me was enough to get them infected.

Every time I ate with them there was always an empty chair that separated them from me. The other kids and I had so much in common, so much to talk about, being an orphan and all. Words couldn't describe how much I wanted to exchange stories with them, but I most certainly didn't. I didn't blame them for the way they acted toward me. I could have acted just like them if one of them were in my place. They were not educated about a disease like HIV. Even at school, we were told that you could get the disease from contact with an infected person. They warned us to keep our distance if we ever found ourselves next to someone who has it. Sitting in the classroom and hearing my teacher talk about a disease that I was currently going through made me suicidal. I have never felt so alone. Everyone was against me because an evil man had chosen to make me his victim.

The school didn't know that I was sick. I'm sure the teachers had made assumptions of some sort of illness, but never would they guess that it was to that extent. My biology professor spent less than fifteen minutes on the topic of HIV. She told us that we were too young to know about HIV, and then she persisted on speaking vaguely about it. Had she continued, I would have wanted to know some facts about the killer who had taken me away from society at such an early age. She mentioned HIV was one of the deadliest diseases among women and men here in our overpopulated town. It has no cure, and we have very little resources to prevent the spread of it.

"For all you young people in here, abstinence is the key to staying HIV free. Once you have it, you will never get rid of it. When it progresses into AIDS then your immune system is done. That stage then becomes the stage of death."

I'm sitting in front of the classroom, knowing that I was going through the things being spoken of, trying to hold my breath and grasping the information that was being said of my illness. She also told us that we didn't have to worry about it right now because we were too young to get it. We knew very little of the disease and very little about sex. She saw no point on wasting time teaching us about something that was no value to some of us. "It was not important to know about it." Those were her exact words. It was not important to the others, but it was important that I knew about it because I was silently going through it. She made assumptions. That's what I didn't want to learn at her short little lectures. My teachers were all arrogant. No wonder the other orphans were this inconsiderate. When you get paid less than four hundred dollars a month, it was okay to teach whatever it is you wanted your students to know.

What my housemates knew was what was being taught in school, which was extremely little. They had very limited knowledge of the disease, and no one was bold enough to change. I have tried numerous times to tell them that the only way you could get infected was through bodily fluids, but no—if they even somewhat touched me it was enough for them to get sick. And if I was taking my medications accordingly, everything would fine. They had nothing to worry about; they chose to make me a worry. Ryan said, "What do you know? You're dumb. We all want you to find a different orphanage to spend the rest of the time you have left." He was always quick to make a statement. It's his friend who says this or that. "That's not true. My friend says not to get close to you because I could get your disease, and my teacher also says the same thing. Why do you think no one likes you or that you have no friends? That's because they don't want to get in contact with you. They're afraid you might kill them, just like you going to die in less than four months." When did he get this fresh? He used to be such a blithe little frail boy. He had a reason to be mad at me. He was unhappy because my being HIV positive had Carole taking another job besides caring for us. Carole no longer gave him the extra care he required. Now that she had two jobs, it was up to him to make sure he was taken care of. Everyone at the orphanage had to look after themselves. With his new demeanor, he can easily be compared to Christina and Rodney. He was just as cruel and mean to me as they were.

Feeling lonely, Christina was nice enough that she was the only kid in the house who volunteered to be my friend. She had clarified what I needed to do in order to consider herself a friend, a friend I would pretty much do anything to keep. At school she wanted nothing to do with me, and at home I was basically begging at her feet to be her friend. I would do anything she asked of me. I did her homework for her while I wore the itchy gloves that left my hand swollen. I think I had an allergic reaction to them. When confronting her about the gloves, she says, "It's nothing. It will go away after you're finish." I washed her laundry for her, wearing the same gloves that left my hand swollen each time I reused them. I'd sit in the dark washing and rinsing and making sure I'd wake up early before the sun rises to hang them up outside for drying before anyone else wakes up. There were times when I just wash her clothes, and she'd tell me to leave the rinsing part for her. The reason is of course she was afraid of her clothes getting contaminated by my disease. I also acted like her personal assistant, reminding her not to forget her make up bag for school. At the end I learned something valuable. I was only her puppet. I was never good enough. She pitied me and I was an obligation to her. I was her personal puppet that she controlled. Forcing someone to be your friend will only leave you broken, nothing more.

I was her charity friend for a while. After school she had gone over her plans on how she was going to find her mother, and I was going to help her find her, and all along she knew she was going to use me. She didn't seem to care much that I was sick and all. Just like I had a goal, she had a goal; the mission was to find her mother. Finally, grasping that the couple weren't coming back for her, she then reinforces another plan. She didn't really speak much about her mother. I think this sudden need to find her mother was her way to get out of the web of lies she was telling her friends at school. Her lies were catching up to her, starting with how early she started coming back to the orphanage and not having Carole pick her up. There was this specific place she wanted to go for the search of her mother. This place was two hours away from Judem

Ville. She was sure that her mother was two hours away from her, north of Judem Ville. She had checked at the school library for directions on how she was going to get there. Directions were not the least of her worries. How were we going to get there? We had no money for a bus. We couldn't walk two hours away. After what happened to me years ago, I was skeptical, scared to ever leave my premises without Carole knowing where I was going. Harmony was the only place that was an exception. I was the only one who knew of her plan. If Nelson finds out, there's a great possibility of getting kicked out of the orphanage. It's a very easy thing for him. I was going to be eighteen in a few months. Any reason was enough reason for him. She constantly reminded me of sworn secrecy. If I told anyone of her plan, she'd disown me as her "secret friend" every day after school. She went over the same plan and studied her directions very frequently. She's planned her search for a while, long before she got me thinking I was a friend. She was scared to follow through with it by herself. That was the main reason she pretended to be my friend in the first place. She needed something, and I was the only one dumb enough to accept her proposal.

The school often has segments about kids getting kidnapped and raped, runaway kids or kids who leave school without adult supervision; those segments got her scared. I wasn't scared. I had already experienced some of the things they've talked about. Their segments always had some truth to it, truth that had already happened to me. I did run away, I did get raped, and I did suffer the consequences of my actions and still am. Runaway kids were more of a target for sex trafficking, something that seize my attention very often with Auntie Annabel, I hated seeing her in such peculiar situation. Seeing her getting in the back of strange men's trucks was a nightmare. Even though she was a grown-up, that didn't exclude her from being a victim. Danger finds its way to anyone. Trucks stop, and she would be inside, not knowing who these people were. It tears me apart that I couldn't do anything to help.

Any talk I had with Christina was in her room. "Pst, pst, come here." She never referred to me by my name. It's always "Hey, pst, you, come here." She knew my name. I think she thought calling me by my name would make me feel like too much of a somebody to her. Christina was a manipulative person, and she was a pro at making people feel less than themselves.

"Do you want to see what I'm going to wear tomorrow?"

"Sure."

I had no interest to stand on my own two feet, staring at her trying her clothes for school. Any activity we somehow did together brought a glower to my face, everything regarding her. Her activities were things to do to make Jasmine more furious. If she was not using me to plan her road trip to a halfway house then I was watching her pick out and try on different clothes to outdo Daphne. She bad-mouthed Daphne any chance she got at the orphanage. It was always Daphne this and Daphne that. It was an ongoing competition between them, and as far as I know Christina was winning. She did get away with Daphne's boyfriend. At school Daphne was no longer the rich girl who gets dropped off by her own chauffeur. Think of it as Christina running Daphne out of business!

"Do you like this?" Even if I did say yes, I like that shirt or that skirt or those shoes or those pair of jeans, she would have ended up wearing something else the next morning. She always does. She undermines me; that's what she does. My say wasn't relevant. I was her puppet, and as coy as I was I did nothing but follow her rules. I went along with everything she did. I was her leading follower. When school was out of session I was the follower who made sure to get her chores done. Wanting to prove to people at the house that Christina was my friend was costing me more than my health. It was costing me the little dignity I had left.

When it came to the battle of popularity in school, Daphne was no longer in the charts. As newbies came into the school, they slowly took over her spot. As the new girls started rolling in, they favored Christina, the attention seeker, the girl who lived in the same orphanage as me, the girl who was controlling me at home and controlling the students who were stupid enough to get manipulated by her at school. When I entered the school, Daphne was the mean girl. She became the only one who was brave enough to stop poking fun at me. As her popularity dived she started to recognize me as a person. As Christina's popularity rose, she became deviated more and more. Daphne had let Christina win the battle. She had Daphne's' boyfriend, and she had Daphne's friends, just like she had told her once before. "I will take everything you own." Daphne's beauty was the only thing that kept her from being treated like me at school. Maybe if her bra size was not a 36C or if her hazel eyes didn't look like Megan Good's with lips that resembled Gabriel Union's or if her body frame didn't look like Naomi Campbell's then maybe we would have more in common. She had the features of the American actresses and models. The reason was maybe because she owned so many magazines of them. She started to look like them too. Her magazines were sort of like her schoolbooks. She paid more attention to them in the back of the classroom rather than the schoolbooks. When I think about it, I can't recall her carrying a schoolbook, ever. She was a rebel. That's what makes her such a big competition to Christina. The professors' "educated" words had no meaning to her.

Daphne had everything that I wished to have. Her body frame was fit to be a supermodel's, and my body frame was fit to look either like a giant or a decrepit girl who could barely walk at times. If she didn't have the beauty, she could have passed for me. Glimpsing at her in the cafeteria, she no longer sat with her puppets, which included four members of the step team, three of the top stars of the soccer team, and the vice president of the junior class. She sat next to the guys who wore black makeup, forcing a word out of them while they gave her angry looks. Daphne used to poke fun at the goth kids in math class, and now that her rich world was crashing down on her, she was begging them to be her friends. She looked scared and confused while trying to peel her orange. She seemed very desperate for companionship. Welcome to the lost world. That was my world. Maybe I could invite her to my world if she wanted to. I would accept her. I had a feeling Daphne would make her way to the bathroom for lunch segments very often, and I was right.

The day Christina wanted me to skip school with her, I had gotten really sick. Still, I had to force myself to go to school. The night before, she made it clear to me that tomorrow was going to be the day she will get her mother back. Nothing could ruin it for her, especially me. We were to leave school around noon to catch the bus early enough to get us back on time to the school property. When I woke up that morning, I was feeling pain in every corner of my brittle bones. She saw that I was hesitant toward getting ready for school. Carole kept track of my appearance. If the blisters started to come back or I grunted the wrong way, she'd demand I stay home. She knew if Carole sees me sick I could stay home from school, which would jeopardize her master plan. To avoid Carole from seeing me, she took my breakfast from Carole and brought it up to my room. I brushed my teeth in my room, and as Carole was using the bathroom, she snuck out of the house, shouting, "We're walking to school." School was only a couple of blocks away. As we started walking I suddenly felt the urge to gag, which left me in a corner vomiting once again. Standing a distance from me, she saw some of her friends walking. She left me in the corner, throwing up, to run after her friends. At that moment I could have easily went back home or made my way to Harmony, but I remembered what she told me. She was my road to making friends in and outside the house, and if I wanted to prove to the kids at the house that I was not a loser who didn't have any friends, I had to stick by her. After my vomiting, I suddenly have no energy. I felt just like three months ago before they found out that I was HIV positive. I struggled to walk to school by myself, which normally wasn't problem for me, but that day after regurgitating on the street, it became a problem. People were staring at me, looking at me oddly. I listened to the other kids talking to their friends about me, about how much of a freak I was, looking the way I did. I saw Christina at the door. She

71

glanced at me and pretended as if she didn't know me. She called me a freak along with her friends while I passed by her. She even joined in the laughter of the other kids mocking me.

My existence didn't matter to anyone, not even the very person I was trying to impress. I was beginning to get it now. No matter what I did I was a lonely orphan infected with HIV, and it was going to stay that way even if I was Christina's' friend or not. I've been to this school for months now. I've watch the new kids come in and out of Valley High, making new friends, forming an alliance and thinking of ways to mock me. I am beginning to understand that I was destined to be the person I am. I was destined to be a rape victim. I was destined to be the orphan at Valley High whom everyone pokes fun of for their entertainment.

I had forgotten to grab my lunch in the rush to get out of the house. In the lunch line, Damian, the most popular boy at school or so I've been told, threw a piece of bread at me. I left my food and ran to the bathroom. Christina followed me there and told me, "Okay, so this is the deal after lunch. This is where we're going to meet. Wait for me at the back entrance. I'll meet you there in about twenty minutes." It's sinking in that Christina was a selfish bitch who only cares about herself. She saw me crying my eyeballs out. Never did she stop and ask me if I was all right. Daphne, who once had the DNA to make my life a living hell, would have never done what she did to me. She once saw me crying in the bathroom and was nice enough to ask me if I was all right. Christina was practically a sister to me. We shared the same home and were close in age, and she had no remorse. She was apathetic, narcissistic.

Who was I to her? I was simply a charity case. She did me a favor by speaking a word to me. I wiped my tears. I went and waited for her at the back entrance just like she told me. As I sat there waiting, I realized I shouldn't care for someone like Christina? Why should I risk being kicked out of the orphanage for someone who didn't even want to be seen with me, for someone who wanted to see me fail, someone who used me no matter what shape I was in, someone who left me on the street vomiting? I must be out of my mind or just plain desperate for her companionship.

Aside from the friendship I was desperately trying to seek, she had nothing else to offer. I left and went to the place where I always felt welcome and comforted, a place where no one was afraid to be seen talking to me. I'd walk a thousand miles to go see Harmony over and over again. I walked a mile to Harmony. It was a mile that made me realize I may or may not have human friends but I had animal friends who were looking out for me, and that's all I needed to be blithe and complete. I got there and they all ran to me in groups. I could hear their voices from a few feet away. Sitting under that peaceful bridge I had already forgotten the humiliation that I had felt at school. I knew she was going to flip out. After all the preparations, I did ruin her chance of seeing her mother, but I didn't care anymore. I stopped caring after Damian threw that piece of bread at me. She was next to him, and she didn't do anything to stop him. I went to the place where I was never judged by my appearance. I went to the place where I was welcomed by the living, where there was constant love and admiration for who I was as an individual.

I had some leftover bread in my bag from two nights ago. I fed the birds, the squirrels, and the swans. I hadn't seen them in so long. Construing the path that I've gone through since I last saw them, they seem to have already known of that chapter. They knew of my illness before I even prepared myself to tell them that I was positive. I explained to them that I was 100 percent sure that I got infected from the man who raped me years ago. For some reason they didn't seem too shocked; they appeared as if they somehow knew the truth already. The swans started whispering to one another, and the birds circled around as if they were about to do some ritual and started singing, humming while forming into a circle around me, whispering words of a different language, a langue that seemed peculiar. My guts tell me something was wrong with them. They seemed out of the ordinary, frightened, and scared. I have never seen them react in such a way before. I lay in the fresh grass, taking deep breaths one after another, in pain but not in pain. I watched my friends shape themselves in a maze silently. Within a minute their maze was formed. I was deep asleep, dreaming about what could never be.

Coming down the stairs of a mansion, people are applauding my descent. I see my mother gazing at me as if I was the most precious thing. People that I've never seen before were there looking up at me, smiling at me. It was strange. The only people who have been so happy to see me in real life weren't people; they were animals of many kinds. But somehow in this dream I was healthy, I was pretty, with thick hair, not brittle thin hair that I shed on my pillows. In this different existence, this tall beautiful girl had the companionship she had long searched for. Getting to the last couple of steps, I stumbled. The same people who were applauding my descent started laughing and pointing fingers at me. That moment got me right back to school. I was reminded of my first day at Judem Valley High. I opened my eyes, screaming "Why!" repeatedly. The Attenders were talking among themselves. I heard them whisper, "Did it work?" They were panicking and talking all at once. With different whispers coming from each one of them, my head started to spin around and my eyes rolled to the back of my head. There was something beyond imagination. Haiti is known for black magic. I start to form my own explanation of these beings. Maybe these beings from nature weren't what they pretended to be. Maybe they were humans that transformed into raptorial forms. They were beyond belief. My mom used to talk to me about Haitian magic. I never took her stories seriously. It went from one ear to the other. As fascinating as her magic stories were, I was too young to even care. She once told me that people who are strong into magic can change themselves from humans to animals of their choice. She once told me when she was a young girl, wandering in the dark streets, she witnessed a woman turning into a cat. Those who can turn themselves into cats are the witches. She told me if I wanted to see strange and unexplained magic, 3:00 a.m. was the time to see that. Her stories were scary and sounded very fictional.

She knew a lot when it comes to the Haitian commitment to voodoo.

Her stories ring a bell to me now. I got weaker once my eyes opened from the vision I had seen. Something mysterious had taken all of my energy, and my blood was pulsing to find out why. I was doing nothing to suddenly feel the way I felt within the short period my brain shut itself from reality. This weakness was not because of my illness. This weakness was deviating. Fearing that I'm in the presence of paranormal activities, I commence to gather my things rapidly. A drop of blood fell out of my nose shortly thereafter. My body felt this aching, sharp pain, a pain I could describe as someone dragging the tip of a syringe needle from my head to my abdominal area, and then it stopped and happened again in the same place. Shortly after experiencing that, my body felt sticky, itchy, and out of proportion. I was sure this was occurring because of my newfound friends. Before meeting them nothing like this has ever happened to me. Did they have some supernatural abilities that I didn't know about? Was this the side effects of the medicines that I had been taking? Impossible. I must be going insane, that's what I thought. How was it that I was able to understand them? I never realized that it was weird that I was able to decipher their language. It struck me that moment as I tried to wipe the line of blood coming out of my nostril.

Another thing that struck me was I fell asleep too quickly. That rarely happened at the orphanage. It took me hours before I could fall asleep. The minute I laid my body on the grass, I was gone, deep in sleep. The dream was weird, too weird, I tell you. It has been a while since I dreamt. I only had nightmares. That's what my brain had come to familiarize itself with since that man violated me. If they were using their supernatural abilities to help me, why the humiliation at the end? Were they trying to send me a message? The biggest question of all—was it coincidence that I stumbled into this place the way I did?

These questions needed answers. Another thing I had noticed after I woke up was that the grass went from this beautiful light green to this dark crumbled dry grass that I had never seen before.

A lot of changes had occurred to Harmony during only a four-hour period. Those four hours were short. How could I sleep for that long without waking up once? If I didn't fall down the stairs, I could have slept till dawn. I always wake up, even if I was forcing myself to take a short nap. The Lucid were flying in circles, and the squirrels were nowhere to be found. I look around, and everything was no longer what it seemed. Harmony was encircled with aged vines that were not present during my earlier visits or before I fell asleep. Out of my mind, scared, I ran with my hands in my nose, trying to figure out what had happened. Running, I bumped into a couple who was running with their dogs. They were running in the direction of Harmony. I ran back, pretending as if I was exercising also. They ran under Harmony as if it was no extraordinary thing. I saw the animals standing still in the path of the couple's direction. They ran right through the animals as if nothing was there. The dog started barking at the animals. The couple pulled the dog with force but was unable to contain it. The dog continued to bark even louder while the animals stood in circles. Finally, after pulling extremely hard, the couple was able to get the dog away from the circled animals. I watched the couple, stumped, while they passed through the animals as if nothing was there. Unbelievably, the dog could see the animals. I could see the animals but the couple couldn't. I was either getting more delusional or they really were paranormal.

As the couple pulled back, I pulled back, running away from them. I walked fast, wanting to be in my clustered room to digest what had just occurred. It was a freak paranormal activity that I was in the midst of. My little web got even more complicated. I couldn't stop going there. That was my place of peace. A new discovery was not going to be a reason to discontinue the little things that were a source of my enjoyment.

Being an hour late back to the orphanage got Carole thinking I ran away again. Since my arrival at this orphanage, I had never been late. "Where have you been? You have me calling Officer Peter to start a search on you."

Officer Peter was the officer who classified me as a runaway girl, the police who introduced me to Carole.

"I'm sorry. I stayed at the library to get some of my homework done."

She looked at me and said, "Don't ever do something like that again. You got me worried, Jasmine. At any time you're staying at the library, please let Christina know. Now go to your room. I'll bring your rice and beans to you shortly."

Straight after school if Carole couldn't pick me up, I would walk home, and if I did skip school, I always left Harmony early enough to make it back to the school yard on time if she was picking Christina and I up. Seeing Carole standing in the front porch with her hands covering her mouth, asking me, "Where have you been, Jasmine?" had me thinking of being more careful next time. Getting kicked out of that orphanage was never a choice. I questioned why Christina didn't say anything to her. She was in the kitchen listening. She had a gift for eavesdropping on people's conversation. In my room I heard her telling Carole that everyone hated me at school. "Behind her back they spoke about her illness. And there's suspicion flowing around the school that she's positive."

"You didn't tell anyone at school she's positive, right?"

"No!"

"You know if you tell, they'll expel her, and she will also be kicked out of this house. Now I don't think that's what you want."

"I'm telling you, I've told no one. Who's to say she didn't tell them herself? It's just talk, people talk."

"Okay, I believe you now."

In the beginning I forced myself to puke to be skinny. She had mentioned that one of her friends had made a comment about me being raped and was now suffering with AIDS or that I was a cancer patient. They made many speculations. My schoolmates were ignorant and apathetic toward people dealing with deadly diseases. They saw you as target for spreading diseases to their kind. They separated themselves from what they thought was the weakest link.

Carole called me back from my room and asked me if what Christina told her were true. It was true; some of their assumptions were true, except I was not a cancer patient nor was I dealing with an eating disorder. I was sure Christina had told one of her friends about my illness, and now it was being passed around the school from mouth to mouth. After minutes of getting a lecture from Carole, I went back to my room thinking about Christina. With the look I was getting from Christina, I knew that something else was coming my way. Knowing how Christina can be, there was no way that she would have let me off the hook for ruining her plan of getting her mother back, at least that's what she thought. She thought skipping school to go find her mother at a halfway house with no chance of getting back to the orphanage on time was her ticket to leave Nelson's orphanage before turning eighteen. She knew very little about disobeying the rules of the orphanage. Rules were rules at the orphanage, and they were to be followed. It's not very easy to find a new orphanage to live once you've been thrown out. I've seen that from the kids I used to hang out with back in the day, the ones who used me to steal food for them. The hard pavement was their bed, and getting thrown out would leave you with just that. You suddenly become a thief struggling for survival in the dark streets. Christina was clueless.

When I was fresh in the orphanage system, going from one orphanage to the other, I had witnessed couples and newlyweds who wanted to start their own family coming into the orphanages and picking the orphans that best suited their lifestyles. The pretty one was often the chosen one to leave with the riches. I never had my hopes up for them anyway. Coming into the orphanage, they knew which direction they were going take. Christina was very close to being chosen, and often she holds the other kids accountable for not being picked. At the dinner table she never holds anything back. Her mouth was her weapon, and she was not afraid to use it. She picks fights with them often.

"You guys will never come close to being chosen. If it wasn't for you delinquents, for all I know I could be in America eating better food rather than rice and beans for breakfast, lunch, and dinner."

"We all struggle here, but Carole does her best to put rice and beans on the table for us every day. You think the little money Mr. Nelson gives to us is enough? It's never enough! Carole is the person we should give thanks to," Nicole says to Christina.

"I don't know about you, but I do not want to eat rice and beans every single freaking day! I'm tired of it!"

"Well, if you're tired of it, don't eat it. I'm sure Ryan could use some more," Natalie says.

"Rice and beans is all she can get for us. If you haven't noticed, our charity money isn't coming in as often as it used to. Rice and beans is still food! You wonder why you didn't get chosen," Evline said.

"I didn't get chosen because of you. You're all just jealous because Mr. Nelson gives me money sometimes to buy food at school."

"Really, I didn't know that! You're so special, aren't you, Christina?" Natalie replied.

"I'm not going to stand for this. You all can go burn in hell."

She got up, pushed her rice and beans toward Ryan, and ran to her room. Carole was at the grocery store running some errands. When she got back, everyone told her that Christina was upset about her meal. Christina was right about eating the same thing every day, but she had no right trying to turn the other kids against Carole. I knew well where she was going with her conversations. As a girl who has the background of moving from one foster home to another foster home, I knew what to do when I wanted to turn my mates against the moms. I once even tried this food game she was playing. In the kitchen, washing my dinner plate, Carole was upset about hearing that Christina was talking bad about her rice and beans.

"Now I'm tired of all this. I have no kids of my own, but yet I feel the need to work extra hard so I can provide for you guys. What is it I'm doing wrong for you guys to think this way?"

"Well, it's not us, Carole. It's Christina. She's trying to turn us against you, I think," Natalie says.

"Now all of you go on, go to your room, and I'll clean this place up."

"Christina says Mr. Nelson gives her spending money. Is that true? How come he doesn't give us spending money, Carole?" said Ryan. He was very little and didn't look a bit his age, but yet he was so smart. His brain capability didn't match his little deformed body. He walks inversely, twisted like any other I've seen, but yet he had the mental capacity of an educated teacher. He was getting even smarter each day.

"I don't know. That is something I'm just going to have a talk about with Mr. Nelson. Now go on now, off you go to bed."

Nicole told Carole that Mr. Nelson was giving Christina spending money behind her back. None of us was given spending money. We have never gotten spending money. We were always told the money coming in was to make sure we take care of the house bills and, most importantly, to make sure we were fed every day.

"What are you doing in the kitchen? What if Mr. Nelson walks in right now and sees you looking this way. Now what am I going to say to him? We cannot afford getting exposed."

"I was just washing my hands."

"Please, just listen to what I say to you, Jasmine. I wouldn't want you to get kicked out of the orphanage, knowing your condition. Now please if you need anything, just wait for me in your room."

I understand clearly where she was coming from. She wanted to keep her job, and I wanted to have a place to stay. Following her rules was the only way to keep what we both wanted. Like before, shortly after eating my dinner, the need to vomit circled through my veins. I ran to the bathroom, throwing up blood and food. The medication had reached its course, leaving me right back to where I started. Taking my medications had given me a break for a while, and now it appeared that the medications had completely lost its value. I wasn't supposed to use the bathroom. The other kids used it, but I had no choice. It was quickest. Carole ran after me to accompany me to the toilet. I could hear the other kids murmuring things about me. I can understand why they hated me so much. Since I came to the house, Carole had put much of the attention they used to get from her on me. Even Ryan was getting less attention; as little and frail as he was, even he couldn't stand me. The less attention he received from Carole, the frailer he appeared to be. Carole's love was what kept him hyper. He became a wanderer, quiet, and most of the time isolated himself in the kitchen corner with Natalie. They shared a little space near the kitchen together, with only a little curtain separating them from the bathroom. They could hear everything that was going on with me; they all could. Who was I to take their "mom" away from them? Before I came to the house, Marlene had told me everyone got along with one another. She told me that the house would have been better without me. In the bathroom I made a request for Carole to stop taking care of me. I didn't mean to act fresh or mean to her, but after reflecting on how the kids felt about me, I had no choice but to bring back the old Jasmine Pierce, the rebellious one. I pulled a fast one on her.

"Please, just leave me alone, Carole! I don't need you here telling me I'm contaminating the toilet with my disease. Say it! I know you want me to walk outside in the dark to do this. Well, I can't! As a matter of fact, I'm going to take my pants off and defecate in this toilet!"

"Let's not worry about this right now, Jasmine. There's more blood in here than food. This is getting out of control."

"Well, there's nothing I can do about it. Leave! I can take care of this on my own. I don't need your pity help!"

In the bathroom, as Carole made an attempt to pull my hair from getting drenched with my vomit, I told her, "Get away from me. For the last time I don't need your help. What don't you get? Are you inane?"

"What has gotten into you?"

"I'm telling you I can take care of myself, but you're not getting it. When I was getting raped, where were you? I didn't need you then, and I certainly do not need you now. I've been taking care of myself for years. Leave me alone!" I pushed her out of the door, slammed the door into her face, and locked it with the vomit splurging across my face while crying and screaming "I don't need you" repeatedly. I was a liar. I did need her, and I never needed anybody beside my mother more than I needed her. She was the only person genuine enough to give me a second chance.

I cleaned up myself and walked head down past the kitchen, where Ryan and Natalie were faking their sleep. In the corner of my blurry eye, I saw Natalie slanting the curtain, watching me take a walk down the shame lane. I went straight into my little corner, crying and feeling sorry for myself, sorry for the way I had misspoken to the woman who only wanted the best for me. Carole was not my biological mother, yet there was a bond between her and I. She knew me better than I knew myself. Unlike the people I had surrounded myself with, Carole was kind. Screaming my name down the corridor of my room, she hugged and walked me to my room. Regardless of my illness, Carole was not afraid if my tears somehow rubbed against her clothes or if my body collided into hers. In the beginning she was. Toward the midst of it all, her knowledge about the disease changed. In my vulnerable moments or at my strongest points, she reminded me of my animal friends. They wanted to show me that I was not alone. As a senile person, it was very difficult to find friends who weren't judgmental of my appearance or my illness.

"Don't think I have forgotten what happened to you. It hurts so much to even think of someone hurting you the way they did. I don't want to hurt you, Jasmine. I want to help you get better, and I can only do that by you conversing with me, letting me offer you help."

"I don't have anything to talk about."

"You need to talk to someone about what you told the doctor and I. I know you briefly told us that you were raped. The doctor had told me that if you have never had sex, the only way you could have caught this disease was from the man who raped you. I want to hear what happened exactly so can I can aid you in finding some closure in this."

"What I told you and the doctor is the truth."

"I know it's the truth, Jasmine, but I need to know how it happened. You're not the only one suffering from this. Every night I go to bed, and all that's keeping me from sleeping is the thought of how someone has hurt you so critically. Just like you need to find closure, I also need to find closure in all of this. I don't know how to help you if you won't let me in."

Up from my bed, I wiped my tears and experienced the horrific horror all over again as I tried to tell Carole of what's been haunting me all these years, of what's been keeping me from what's really important in life. It was a dark night I will never forget. I was in a wrong place at the wrong time. It was one of those nights when I had a habit of sneaking out of the orphanage. I was walking in a dark alley with my hands in my coat pocket when out of nowhere I sensed that someone was walking behind me. Looking back, I saw no one. However, I sensed there was someone following me. The footsteps got louder as I walked faster. At some point I ignored the noises in the back of me. Each time I heard the footsteps, I'd walk faster. The alley was always free of people late at night, and I was aware of that. I wasn't afraid of walking the streets late at night. It wasn't till that night I started fearing the streets. That night was not the first time I had walked alone in that alley. I always came back safe. That alley was a place to escape my emptiness until that night. It became the place of fear no matter what street I was in. When I felt the footsteps getting closer to me, I proceeded to look back again, only this time the man was right in the back of me. Disconnected from the streets that I often walked in, I no longer knew where I was. My brain shut itself out completely from defending myself. I was hit by a big surprise, let me tell you. When he grabbed me I didn't even have time to defend myself. He grabbed me with force. He transported me to a secluded area, an area where no one could hear or see me. I was trapped. I yelled for help but no one came for me. When my screaming got too loud, he took his jacket and wrapped my head with it. I tried to fight him off, but he was too strong. Under his hands I was left paralyzed to defend myself. I couldn't escape. I begged him and pleaded with him to stop, but he wouldn't. He won I lost complete control of myself. lying on the cold ground, death could have taken its course. At that point I didn't care if I lived to see another day. Once he was done, I was left in the cold, paralyzed, and I was no longer able to scream. I fell into a deep sleep, a coma it felt like. A woman who was on her way to work found me lying on the cold pavement and shook me up. She seemed very familiar as if she had done this before. It was very likely that she has woken someone from sleeping on the streets. For some of us the streets were a home.

When she realized how disarrayed I was, she said to me, "Good God, what has happened to you?" My pants were halfway down my knees, my shirt was torn apart with the buttons missing, one shoe was on my foot and one was a distance from me. The barrettes in my hair were missing, leaving my hair to collect dust parts for the lady to remove. When the lady handed me my pants, there was a significant amount of bloodstain on them. She asked me if I wanted to go to the hospital, but I refused. I told her, "I'll be all right." Go to the hospital for what? Only for them to remind me of how poor I was? No, I was good. As I searched for the missing shoe, I took a glance back at where I was left for dead and said to myself, "You have taken everything I had left." This is the mistake that I have to live with for the rest of my life. Every time I have a flashback of this night, it feels like I'm living that night over again. I hate that I have no control over my nightmares or my flashbacks.

"Do you remember how this man looks like?" Carole asked me.

"It was so dark that I didn't get the chance to see his face. Even in my nightmares I can't see his face. It's always covered in darkness. He haunts me everywhere I am, and he laughs at me."

Carole left the room exasperated. She begins to take it out on the other kids. From my room I could her screaming at the other kids to go to bed once again. She found them running away from my door. They were listening to our conversation.

"If I have to ask you kids to go bed again, disciplinary actions will be taking place. I'm tired of repeating myself to you kids!"

It was only nine o'clock. Something else must have been bothering Carole; it was seven when she told them to go to bed. We never had to go to bed that early. We chose when we go to bed. There was never anything else to do after dinner, so we all prepared ourselves for bed without being asked. The only times Carole asked us to go to bed was when the other kids were arguing, not when the whole house was in silence after they have mocked me of my illness. Maybe working two jobs and watching out for thirteen different kids were finally catching up to her. Never have I seen this side of Carole before. She got so livid and I was the reason for it. I have given the other kids more reason to despise me. In my room, enveloped in fear, I could feel the house shaking from everyone rushing to their locations.

Hearing about the root of the nightmare that has turned my world upside down, Carole's outlook changed. Being a humble person was not the only side of her. Yelling and disrespecting her in the bathroom was nothing to her. She was used to this kind behavior, especially from Christina. Yelling at her was not something that could get her upset, but my struggle did. It was enough to bring the bad in her. This incident became too much for her to handle. She had problems of her own, and now I was adding to it.

Within minutes all I heard was silence. Everyone had gone to their corners. I tried to close my eyes, but telling the story to Carole had triggered my memory completely. The flashbacks wouldn't stop coming. I began to see the man making a mockery of me once again. My mind was deceiving me. I was seeing things as if it was actually happening at that moment. I was frozen and helpless. The door creaked, and it took me a while to see that it was Christina standing in front of me. Not knowing it was her standing in front of me, I saw her as my rapist. I was begging him to please not hurt me. When Christina finally said something, I rapidly refrained from pleading.

"I don't know what kind of stunt you're trying to pull here. Whatever it is, it needs to stop," Christina said to me lividly.

All of a sudden I see Marlene, Nicole, Rodney, and Ryan coming, telling me that I needed to leave the house. I understood deeply what they were feeling. I was taking their spotlight off of them; it was time that they regain it. Little old me came to the house taking all the attention from them. My time was up. They all came to me with anger and rage, wanting to take back what was theirs. They no longer wanted to see me in their house, regardless of the circumstance, and I had no say in it. Looking at them rambling all at once I got up to leave the room. I was tired, and blood would not stop coming out of my nose once again. As they saw me coming toward their direction with a bleeding nose, they all quickly moved aside. I'm happy to see that it took me to bring them together. They all had one thing in common. They all didn't want their bodies to come in contact with me, and it was clear to me. No one wanted me, Jasmine Pierce, around. Nineteen seventy-three was the year of the ignorant and the uneducated. They made you feel low. I couldn't possibly feel any worse than what these kids have been trying to make me feel. When I thought they couldn't get the worst of me, here they go proving me wrong.

I gave them my room and went outside in the dark to keep my bodily fluids from spreading into the orphanage. I lay on the ground with paper towels, pressing it against my nose to keep the blood from coming. There I go thinking how I was one step backward in trying to make them like me. I was done trying to make them like me. Nothing I did changed their minds. All I was to them was "a complainer, an attention seeker, and a no one." Could you ever change someone's mind from thinking this way, especially if they were children?

Outside on the pavement with a bloody nose, my frail body had given up on the effort to defend itself. Mark, who wakes up often in the middle of the night to use the toilet, saw the door open. As he made an attempt to close the porch door, he heard a cough, a cough that was coming from me. He saw my frail body shivering, in dire need of warmth and comfort. He took my hand and helped me find my way to my now-empty room. Getting into bed was tough, but Mark helped me. Shivering, he covered my body with the comforter; he told me that everything was going to be fine, wanting nothing in return. Everyone who entered my room besides Carole needed something from me. Marc was different. He was another concerned soul that I've come to know at the orphanage, and I had never seen this side of him before mainly because he was often busy fighting with the others, and when he was not fighting he was sitting in the living room, forcing his eyes to watch static movies. He was not concerned by much. He was the only one who didn't vote for me to move out of the house. When the other kids came to my room, ordering me to leave the orphanage, he was in his corner, lying on the floor watching his movies.

When it comes to girls, Mark gets a little shy around them. He and I had something in common. We get really uncertain when it comes to the opposite sex. My uncertainty was because of hate and anger. He never looks up when he talks to me. Unlike the others, never has he shown hate toward me. Our relationship was neither cold nor warm, and after what he did for me that night, he had become one of the few people in my life who saw me for something else beside my illness. The others have been very bad-mouthing me, and at some point he was starting to believe them. From the beginning they have told him, especially Christina, the queen of "perfect," that I was infected; and if he were to come near me, he himself would be infected.

As the medications reached the end line, the more I find myself staying alone at the orphanage, contemplating on how to leave. That's what everyone's been wishing for. It was time to think about them. I had nothing but time in my hands. Sitting home alone, time dragged. Thinking was all I did. I thought maybe I could leave and head south toward where my mom was buried. I could find her burial ground and stay there with her. At least there I'd be with her. I even thought of going back to where my mother used to work and ask for a job at the clothing factory. That was my thoroughly calculated plan, to head back to Gonaives and work where my mother's soul might still exist.

Dear Carole, if you're reading this I'm probably gone by now. Please don't look for me, for I will be home at the place where I was nurtured by my mother. Thank you, everyone, for accepting me into your orphanage. By reading this I hope you see that I'm doing what is best for everyone. Since my arrival here, I have been nothing but a heavy mallet. With me being here, it will only make everything more severe. Stay strong, everyone.

I didn't take much with me, only a piece of half-eaten bread that was sitting on the table and some sugar and two bottles of water for the equivalent of juice. Shortly after putting my foot outside the porch I collapsed to the ground. I tried to reframe myself but couldn't. I felt numb and unable to get up. Taking a deep breath suddenly became work. My breathing became shallow and slow. I could no longer feel my heart beating. No one was around. If I leave the orphanage, who will catch me? I needed Carole and the little charity money that was coming in once in a while. I needed to receive some part of it, especially being in the condition I was in. I couldn't leave the orphanage. The other kids may have been merciless, but it was my second home. I simply needed to stay out of their way. Staying out of the other kids' way suddenly became my top idea. If I was to stay there until my time, it was the only way I could at least die peacefully. Leaving like this could bring me right back to where I started, being classified as a runaway, and who knows, I might not get the job, and even if I did I couldn't keep it because of my illness. It is constantly disabling me from doing almost everything. Every now and then I find myself staying at the orphanage because of it. I couldn't go to school. I couldn't walk around the neighborhood without being judged. This decision to leave the orphanage couldn't be followed through after strongly considering. Collapsing was a sign of the obvious. Without Carole, I couldn't survive on my own.

I took the note and tore it with anger and force and sat back at the table.

Promising to stay out of the other orphans' way became my job. If I wanted to stop hearing "you're not needed," I needed to start feeling needed. I started to get more involved around the house while staying out of their way. Watching them going up and down, getting ready for school, I asked, "Do you need help with anything?" With her mind seemed lost, she said, "Go wash your hands, and put everyone's lunch in their bag, will you, please?"

"Yes, Carole."

It felt good hearing those words coming out of her mouth. I was ready, expecting a no from her. She was in a rush; everyone was in a rush. That yes could have possibly been a no, but who knows. I was happy being in the kitchen, lending her a helping hand, considering she has been doing just that for me.

"Jasmine, can you please pass me the sugar? I need to make some juice for Ryan."

I rushed to the kitchen, passing her the sugar to make sugar and water for Ryan. Sugar and water was what I called her juice. Once the drink was made, Ryan grabbed his lunch bag with a piece of buttered bread in his hand to eat on his way. I asked him, "Hey, Ryan, do you want someone to walk you to school?"

As he placed the bread into his mouth, he shrugged his shoulders together against his neck, saying, "Mmkay, but only if you want to."

"I don't mind walking you. Wait for me. I'm going to ask Carole if I can."

"Carole, do you mind if I walk Ryan to school?" I asked her.

In her busy work mode, she says, "Sure, just be careful walking back."

"All right, let's go, she says I can," I said to Ryan.

Now Ryan didn't go to a regular school like the rest of us. He was the youngest one in the house. Only eight years of age, the orphanage couldn't afford sending him to a private school. There weren't any public schools for his age. The public schools started with ages ten and up. Lucky for Ryan, he was not the only one around the block who was underage for public education. Not too far away from the orphanage there was an organization that teaches the younger ones. This organization was in multiple tents placed near a little farm where Carole's second job is. The owner of the farm was the one who formed this organization. Because of them, now Ryan and so many others didn't have to stay home while they watched their older siblings go to school.

"Can I ask you a question?" I attempt to start a conversation with Ryan.

"Sure. What is it?"

"Why do you guys gang up on me so much?"

"We're not trying to gang up on you. Well, at least I'm not. Maybe. I don't know. It's just that since you got here, Carole appears to care more about you than us."

"I think she cares about all of us equally."

"No, that's not true. We see how she's quick to react when you grunt."

"It's only because I'm really sick, and I may die very soon."

"Well, I know that. I miss her, Jasmine. Just like she's the only one you got, she's the only I've got too, ya know," he says to me when I made a move to grab he's hand as he crossed the street. He was still aware of my disease. He pulled his hand away from my hand and said, "Well, I'm here now. Thanks for walking me to school."

"No problem. Anytime, buddy," I said back to him.

"Maybe when you don't go to school, you can walk me to school again."

"And I would love that."

"Bye now."

Walking back to the orphanage, that's all I needed to end my day. My heart just opened up and let the air of agony out. That day was when I made a little brother. These words spoken, they weren't the greatest words, but they were uplifting, soothing, and were all I needed to feel welcome. We all were going through a tough era. Some of us bottle them up inside, which turns the heart into coal; and some of us, like me for instance, just want someone to talk to while going through this time of hardship. Ryan was young; he may not fully understand what was going on at the orphanage or understand the capacity of my disease, but he was a smart kid who knew what he was missing, a smart kid who knows why he is living in a house packed with thirteen kids, struggling to keep his food from being taken by the others. He also knew why he wakes up every morning, only to find himself going to school in a tent while his best friend, who's younger than him, goes to his fancy school.

He asked him, "How come I never see you at my school?"

It was sad for all of us. If we worked together it could have been less of a sad situation for all of us, but instead we took it out on each other. It's too late now to correct the mistake that's been made.

Carole works less at the farm as I appear to need more of her guidance each day. I was out of money, out of medications, and out of time. Death was approaching; it was around the corner, waiting for me to take my last breath, and I no longer wanted that for myself, as I regained a brother. Getting closer to the magic age, eighteen, Mr. Nelson tells me the moving-out days are getting closer. Mr. Nelson started coming to the orphanage more often than usual. He was getting suspicious that I may need more of his money for the hospital. I think deep down inside he knew I was sick. Bringing the conversation out may have forced him to do what's right. When it comes to doing what's right, he didn't have a clue about it, especially if it involves his money.

Christina was closer to her magic age also, but yet I was the one getting the boot. He was giving Carole ultimatums about my exiting the orphanage. In fact I can't ever recall him giving Carole a hard time when it comes to Christina. As my magic age approaches, Carole was getting less money for my stay. During a confrontational conversation between Mr. Nelson and Carole, I overheard them talking about the thing that I lack most and money. "Eighty will not suffice for a month. Lately she's been the only one getting this little money."

"If you think it's not enough then make it enough!" Mr. Nelson says to Carole lividly.

"I wasn't planning on telling you this. I think if you hear this you'll allow yourself to help her. She needs our aid."

"Whatever it is, I don't want to know. No, no, and no!"

"Hear me out, Mr. Nelson. I should have told you this a long time ago, when it was first discovered."

"Whatever you want to tell me, I already know about it. Don't think I didn't know."

"You knew? And all this time you've done nothing. Instead you come over here with eighty dollars. This poor girl has been through a lot, Mr. Nelson!"

"Everyone has been through a lot. What we do is we deal with it!"

"Why are you this way, Mr. Nelson? I look at you and I see a person that needs a heart. How can you be this cold, so selfish?"

"I have no heart? I've known she's been HIV positive the first night she spent in the hospital. The doctor notified me. And you think I'm cold! I should have had her thrown out of the orphanage upon her return, but I didn't! 'Bout I show you how cold I can be by asking her to leave right now!" Mr. Nelson couldn't have been any closer to Carole's face. She's pointing her finger at him, he's yelling at her, and in the end there was no wining with none of them. My time was up.

"I trusted you, Carole! The reason I pretended I didn't know of Jasmine is because I thought you respected me. I wanted you to come to me and tell me yourself and you didn't. I should have you out with her. You seem to want to protect her so much," Mr. Nelson said intensely.

"What do you want to do, huh? You have it all figured out!"

"I don't know! I just don't know! I need to think," he said to Carole as he stepped back from her.

"I'm an old lady. These youngsters are the only people I've got. If you want to take that away from me, go ahead. I have nothing to fight for but these children."

"Jasmine can't stay here," said Mr. Nelson.

"Where is she going to go? She's very ill, Mr. Nelson. She has nowhere else to go."

"You find something."

"I know the law, Mr. Nelson. She still has a few months left before she turns eighteen. I know a thing or two about the law."

She did know a thing or two about the law. The matter was she was a woman. She could protest and argue with the system, but they would never take her side no matter how hard she tried. Women have no say, and it's been that way for years. The men like the power too much to let it slip away to women with strong voices.

"I have no problem leaving with her if that's what it takes to help her. If I leave, the question is can you take care of the eleven kids left behind? You don't know the first thing when it comes to children!"

"All right, all right, I'll let her stay here, but I better not see her face when I come here! If I see her, she's out. And another thing she will no longer get funds. I'll see how you'll provide for her. She's in your hands now!"

"You will not die a happy death, old fool. You will not die a happy death, I tell you," Carole says to Mr. Nelson as she gazes into his eyes.

"And you will die of HIV. She'll pass it on to you, mark my words. The girl that you'll die for is a whore. She's the only young girl I know around here who has a disease like this! Why should I waste my time on someone who's going to die no matter what I do?"

"Did the doctor also tell you that she was raped?"

"Yeah, he did, and he's not buying her story. Carole, think about it, she was found on the streets, she had no parental supervision, no one knows. The girl was a prostitute, I tell you. That's the only place you can get a disease like this!"

"And you believe him?"

"Of course I do. I feel bad for that poor man she's accused!"

"You have kids of your own. What would you do if this was one of your kids, Mr. Nelson?"

"This would never or will be one of my kids. I didn't raise them to be sluts. Now where's Christina? I don't have time for your shenanigans!

"Christina!" Mr. Nelson yells for Christina. "Where's Christina? I want to talk to her!"

"Coming," Christina replied to him.

Christina ran to the front porch, for he was waiting there for her. Watching this playing out in front of my eyes, the guessing, the questions, and the maybes have been answered. It became clear to me that Christina was Mr. Nelson's favorite. All the guessing, all the assumptions stopped there.

"You called me?" Christina said to Mr. Nelson as she approached him. He got down to her height, held both her arms firmly, and said to her, "Now I have a job for you. Do you want a job?"

"Yes! What kind of job is it, Mr. Nelson?"

"I want you to make sure Ms. Carole is not using your money to provide for that girl Jasmine. Stay away from her too, I beg of you."

Even to him I was just that girl. I couldn't possibly be anything else. "Now here's a little money for your trouble. Go ahead now, I'll see you soon."

"Thank you, Mr. Nelson." She hugged him good-bye.

What would it take for me to get this much love from him? I see now why Christina's room was so special. I see why she was the way she was. What would it take for me to get this special attention from Mr. Nelson? Would it take changing my looks for him? I believe it would. That was never going to happen. The rumors were not rumors. While we all suffered for food, Christina rejoiced in the power that her beauty has. Mr. Nelson treated her as if she was his own.

Christina didn't like me. Now she had another reason to dislike me. She had a job, and her job was to make sure she watched me struggle. She was reporting to the money-hungry man, Mr. Nelson. Afraid of her watching my every move, I stayed in darkness, avoiding clashing into her. This has been my own goal since Mr. Nelson had me under the radar. It's now my job to make sure Christina didn't find me using anyone's funds.

With the one last ninety-eight dollars given to Carole, I had more worries than ever. Any second now, Mr. Nelson could pop into that door and order me to get out. Not a day went by that I didn't think about my living situation. Ninety-eight dollars was not even enough for one of the three medications I was taking, let alone food. I lived by day without hope with Christina watching my every step. She took her job very seriously, adding that she was rooting for me to blink, make a mistake, so she could go report to Mr. Nelson. With no medications left, I was in the worst shape of my life. My eyes were so far into the back of my head that my vision had become impaired. When I looked at myself in the mirror, I could no longer see myself. I was seeing someone that I didn't recognize; this person didn't look a bit like what I was in my adolescent age.

Avoiding the shattered mirror hanging in the bathroom was troubling, for I was catching a glimpse of myself at every turn. Seeing my soul forcing itself to get out of its shell became too familiar. I couldn't stand it anymore. My body itself mocked every bit of me. Often I saw myself appearing as someone else, someone that I could never be. Daphne sometimes appeared as my image even. I even saw myself as Christina from time to time. Everything I wished I could be deceived me. Frequently it was looking at my true self that changed the opinions of many. What I saw in the mirror was what people questioned, not what my mind frame wanted me to believe. The image of Daphne and Christina appearing in the mirror was its way of making me hate myself more.

With only three pills left, death was getting closer than expected, and my ongoing flashbacks were stronger as my medications came to an end. Everything that was going on at the orphanage was working with death. With a team involving Christina, Mr. Nelson, the school system, and everyone else, I might as well give up the battle; and I was ready to give it up if nothing comes to fight with me. Alone and in despair, my lack of hope and faith faded ultimately. I always thought that if I kept taking my medicine then I would be cured of my disease. I didn't really know much about the disease I was suffering from anyway. I talked about the guys being clueless, and there I was standing just as clueless as them.

In an era when people were exposed to various kinds of diseases, HIV was on the list with very little knowledge and treatment for it. Once you were diagnosed with it, your only cure was death. And everyone's mental thinking if you were diagnosed with it was that you were a slut, a prostitute who slept around a lot and don't use protection. Here I am; I was all of the above according to the community. At the age I was when that man forced himself on me, I didn't even know there was such a thing as HIV. I knew nothing of it, and I know little about sex presently. The only thing I know about sex was what my mother told me. Young and in her care, she often told me, "Stay away from men. They're nothing but trouble." Another thing she always used to tell me as she prepared me for school was, "Men only want one thing. They'll tell you everything you want to hear, and once they get it, they'll forget even the thought of you." That statement I carried with me everywhere I go. Part of why I couldn't stand the idea of men was because of my mom. She was right. A mother's instinct is always right. I understand everything now.

I watched her work three different jobs just to take care of both of us. The little time I spent with her, I never saw any man coming to the house. I never met my father. She was both my mother and my father. She did all the things a father did for his child. Aside from her drug habits, she was a great mother. When I couldn't sleep at night, the little good memories I have left of her was what kept me smiling. In spite of everything we've been through, she'll always be my mother, dead or alive. The memories of her replaced hurt with smiles. Seeing her best friend Auntie Annabel on the streets, selling herself short, I try to find ways to help her yet it's still difficult. I can't do much for now, but my triumph will not end here. For now I try not to think about her as much; rather, I picture the good moments we spent together. I picture her teaching me how to cook instead getting into those savage trucks. With everything wrong I saw Aunt Annabel doing in the streets, I replace that image with memorable memories. My mother and Auntie Annabel would've never thought or say that I was a slut.

With Christina and Mr. Nelson watching my every move, my every concern, it left Carole in distress, spending every bit of money she has worked for on my care. "If Mr. Nelson isn't going to help you during your stay here, we need to look for help elsewhere," Carole says to me.

"Can you help me find a job?"

"Ahh! A job! Jasmine, with the way your health is right now, you should be buying your coffin," she said to me while she faked a laugh.

"What can I do, Carole? I can't do anything! Why don't I leave here? That's what's best for everybody."

"It could be. However, I'm not letting you do that. I couldn't live with myself knowing that you left in this condition. I know an arbiter. We're gonna go and find you some aid. How about that?"

"Will they help me?"

"I don't know, but it's worth at try. I'm tired, Jasmine. I can't work at that farm anymore. I'm too old for it. I've spend all that I've made on you. I'm sorry, I need a rest. After we meet with Jack Demieux the rest is up to you."

"Who's Jack, Carole? You never speak of this person," I asked her.

"He's a lawyer who often bends the rules for some people. I've known him for a few years now. I'm sure he will consider taking your case."

Early in the morning, Carole and I headed to court, ready to fight for justice, at least that's what I was thinking. This was my last chance for some support. Carole was tired of helping me, and Mr. Nelson had an army consisting of Christina waiting for any faux pas. I knew for a fact I will never get a job. After this dispute there was nothing else to dig into. Ready for Jack to explain my case I stood no chance; jurors looked at me with grunts.

With Carole standing to the left side of me and Jack to the right I was sure the judge would see my pain. "Your Honor, we're here today because we are strongly in need of your aid."

"What can I do for you, and may I add this girl standing next to you does not look too good?" says the judge.

"Well, she's the reason we're here today. She's currently battling a disease that could take her life very soon. I need you to work in her honor by granting her some funds and the chance to stay at the orphanage longer. I need you to buy her some time," says Jack.

"How old is she?"

"In two months she will be eighteen years of age."

"I don't see how I can help you here. She's almost free to be on her own! Once she leaves the orphanage, she can make plans to get herself a job. Get herself situated, sir."

"You don't understand, Your Honor. She won't make it alone. She's severely ill. She's HIV positive. The doctors only gave her seven months to live. She does not have much time." I looked across the room, and the jurors were stunned by the illness.

"Excuse me, can you repeat what you just said? I'm having a hard time understanding this."

"She has AIDS!" Jack repeats again.

"So you're telling me this . . . this frail, this young girl is dying of a sexually transmitted disease soon. At this early age."

"Yes, and if you don't help her, I'm afraid she won't make it for another month."

"And we all can agree she's been prostituting herself for quite some time. She's an orphan, what can I expect." I looked at everyone laughing as the judge made that remark.

"How many other kids are at the orphanage, sir?"

Carole replied by saying, "Twelve"

"There are a total of thirteen, with her included."

"Do you realize you're risking the other kids' lives by her staying there? What kind of person are you?" the judge asked Carole.

"She has nowhere else to stay, sir!"

Hearing that I had AIDS made them think that I was a troublesome little girl. Being an orphan made them think that I was a parentless teenager who had been sleeping around and eventually ended up with HIV. The judge thought so, and so did everyone else in the court. Going to court had been the worst mistake. Now even authorities were ordering me out of the orphanage.

"What's wrong with you, child? In all my life of being a judge, I have never gotten a case like yours," the judge asked me.

I stood in front of the courtroom, trying to explain to a bunch of strangers what happened to me just so I could get some aid from the corrupted authorities. Explaining or no explaining, they still saw me as a young prostitute dying from HIV. How could I change their minds from thinking the way they did? I did truthfully tell them what had happened to me. They turned my words into lies as I struggled to explain my situation. The jurors screamed, "Prostitute!"

The judge ordered me to stay away as I tried to walk toward his seat. "Stay where you are, miss! Don't come any closer."

"I'll stay here. Is this okay?"

"Fine," said the judge.

"Your Honor, I know what you're thinking. According to you and many other people, I'm a prostitute. I can't stretch that enough. You're sitting in front of a panel trying to make sense of my condition. I was left beaten, raped, and paralyzed in the cold by a man who I've never met in my life. A few years later, doctors are telling me that I'm going to die. I am as shocked as you are. My innocence was brutally taken from me. I was helpless and weak. Till today I am still mad at myself that I wasn't able to defend myself from that man. Standing here today in front of you, all I am asking is for some aid. My time here is very limited, and if you could find a way to make my little time here on Earth less distressful I would greatly appreciate it."

"What do you want me to do for you? I can't do nothing for you. You're almost eighteen, dear. Any help you're getting right now it's coming to an end shortly," the judge said.

"All we need is enough to get her back to her medications. We're not asking you for a million bucks, Your Honor. She has three pills left, and once they're done, the doctor said that her chances of staying alive are going to be very slim," Carole says.

Those three pills should have been gone already. Carole made me save them for harder times.

"If you won't help us, the hospital won't help us, who will? You'd rather watch this innocent little girl die rather than to offer help? The gracious God does not pardon people like you. Evil child you are!"

"Ma'am, there's nothing I can do for her. The only thing I can offer her is my prayers and to wish her the best of luck and for God to bless your soul."

"Please help me! Please!" I cried to the judge.

"Get this prostitute out of my court. Oh and be careful, Bailiff, she might rub her disease against you."

And he banged his gavel, saying, "Court dismissed." That was it. "Court dismissed" was what he said. After he banged his gavel, I proceeded to get a couple of words out, crying out to him, saying, "I don't want to die! You have a say in this matter! Help me, please!" Once I was outside the court after the judge had asked the bailiff to remove us from the courtroom, he then again asked the security guards to escort Carole and I outside. My heart dropped at that moment. Seeing the judge was my only hope. I was sure that they would see my case and offer me some help. Because I was almost eighteen, they saw no reason to still offer me aid. Because I was HIV positive, I was to leave the orphanage. Because I was poor, the authorities abandoned my cries. I was almost 18 years of age, they were happy to know that, once I turn 18 I was out of their care. More power and more money to them.

100

I was one less kid that they no longer needed to help. What help? What I needed help with, the most they avoid.

"I've tried my best to help you, Jasmine. I've tried. Now the court system won't look at your case. I can't say things will get better from here," Carole said as we walked back to the orphanage.

"I know you tried, Carole. I know. If you want me to leave the orphanage, I'll leave. By tomorrow, early morning, I'll be gone," I replied.

"Don't be stupid, Jasmine. You're staying at the orphanage. We just won't tell Mr. Nelson of what occurred today. Don't speak any word of this. You hear me?"

"I promise."

"You are going to be without medications for a while. I'll be using more home medicines for your treatments. You don't worry about a thing, you hear me?"

How she was good to me. Heaven-sent she was. She was an old woman with every trick up her sleeves. She knew everything about everything, from her beloved home medicines to her authentic ways of caring for those close to her. The world may have given up on me, but for as long as I was breathing she was willing to be one of those people who cared for me. I can only imagine what could've been if that police officer didn't stop me on my way to nowhere. I could be dead in a hole somewhere, being identified simply as a number just like my mother. Now dead looking, watching her taking care of Ryan, I can only offer thanks for having her trapped all those months.

To continue on with the story, after my only chance had been drained by the judge, my life was over. I only had two more months till I turned eighteen. There was nothing else left to search for. I have applied for jobs, but when they learned that I was an orphan it disqualified me from that department. Everyone around the neighborhood knew Carole and what she does for a living. She took care of the homeless kids, the orphans, or the unwanted. Putting Carole's name on a job application of mine disqualified me immediately. Most of the places that I have applied to, I have seen students from school working there. Anyone could work at the places that I have applied to, except for me of course. And the fact that I was sick, that was another thing that kept me from having a job. No one outside of the house knew that I was HIV positive. There were only speculations floating around the neighborhood, which worsened things. People couldn't have a kid living with AIDS spreading their disease. Some of these people could've helped me, but they chose not to for their own greedy reasons.

Carole told me that I couldn't work specifically because I was positive. She says I had a greater chance of getting a cold from somebody, or to make matters worse, someone could get infected. I understood that. I wouldn't want nobody to feel the way I did. I wouldn't want them to go through what I was going through. Helping Carole around the orphanage was what I did for the month to compensate for her aid. She was the only person I was getting direct aid from throughout my illness.

Getting it through my head that there was no one to get aid from, I started to help more around the orphanage. I kept the backyard free of animal feces by frequently sweeping. That was a job I kept Carole from doing. I helped her wash the other orphans' clothes while they were away at school. Most of the things she couldn't find time doing, I helped with. By helping out in the house, I'd hope to solicit respect from Mr. Nelson. Maybe if Carole tells him how useful I've been to the orphanage, he'd consider his state of mind toward me. Who was I fooling? Certainly not Mr. Nelson, the grouch.

Running out of time, money, and medicines, I started to adapt myself to what it will be like for me living in the orphanage on my eighteenth birthday if I wasn't dead before then. I started to think of the places I could go. Outside the orphanage I had no other place to go. Every place I thought of had given me a reason to not return back. I could sit and do as much planning as I could; it would bring me to the same end. Sleeping on buses, going back to my old self, stealing food off the merchandisers, and, if I'm lucky, I could go back to those friends that I used to steal for. All my planning for when I leave the orphanage had no happy endings. Maybe I could find a place under Harmony, settle there, and wait for my death. I didn't have much time left by any means, why waste my energy on searching for something that wasn't there? Harmony may have made me nervous, but that was the place I had planned to live at for the time being.

Running out of money, Carole found herself going back to work for the farm in order to provide for me. The little money she had left was far from enough to get one of my HIV medications. Secretly picking out of Christina's spending money she was able to purchased two out of the ten other medications that Dr. Jean had prescribed. With no money, my only source of medication was Carole's herbs, her home remedies. She walks far to get these special kinds of herbs. Since her wagon had given up on her, she has done nothing but walk. With no income for her bus or taxi rides, she found herself walking more often than usual. Her feet were swollen. She didn't pay much attention to that. She didn't complain about her swollen feet. She wakes up early mornings to get things done for us before she makes her way to the farm. She wasn't making much at the farm; she was making only $1.50 a day. Even if she works for two weeks making this amount a day, it wouldn't be enough to get these different meds, but it would be enough to buy herbs, herbs that replace the expensive medications. She makes herbal tea for everyone when she has a good day at the farm. We all knew if she had a good day at work. She has a smile that puts a smile on everyone's faces no matter what shape of sadness we were in. Sometimes she brings chicken parts to make dinner for us. If we look outside and see she has a smile on her face and a bag of chicken pieces in her hand that marks a good day because she is able to cook something other than rice and beans. Her working at the farm again had its advantages; she gets free herbs as compensation for coming in early before everyone else. She was doing everything she could to make end meets.

Another thing I had little recollection of was Carole's home medicines. The stinkier they get, the more comfort I find in them. Her medicines aid well in my comfort; those were what I knew of when it comes to her self-made remedies. The week prior to my death she brought to the orphanage dried leaves of different kinds, for different times of the day. Since I was kept home from school very often, I was given a lot of her treatments. She had the papaya leaves mixed with walnut leaves boiled with a cup of her own oil for the mornings. By the end of the day I was oily, odd smelling, and in great relief. With her home remedies I always felt great afterward but only for a short time. The prescriptions lasted me hours when it came to keeping off the physical suffering. In order to feel the way the prescribed medications made me feel she had to constantly mix different herbs and constantly massage my body with the herbs. She always knew what's right. This tea helped with the cleansing of my body; it also reduced my ongoing fevers. Every morning and before heading to bed I'd have two cups of her tea. It may have been bitter and slimy, but that tea had done so much for me. It was close to the feeling that I got from my prescribed medications. I didn't like the taste much. It was a process drinking that tea; it took time before it eventually made it down to where it needs to be. I'd close my deep brown eyes and pretend the tea was a cold glass of grape Kool-Aid or a cold glass of Carole's sugar and water juice, which always calms my nerves. I loved Kool-Aid, but after I started feeling sick it didn't agree too much with my stomach. Oh how I loved my Kool-Aid. In the beginning I hated the sugar and water ordeal, but the more it was served with dinner, the more I began to enjoy it.

It came to a point where even the herbs were no longer helping. Sometimes sitting in my room and feeling like something was eating away at my stomach was part of the reason the humming noise wouldn't stop at night. Carole's tea used to help me with the constant stomachache; even that stopped working. I no longer carried a weight anymore. My organs started to eat away at itself. There was this constant churning and pain flowing through my body that wasn't going away. What brought tears to my eyes wasn't the idea of being ill or friendless. It was not even the pain or the fading of my image. It was the fact that I longed to see my mother. She wasn't there to tell me the location of my father.

Although I never asked of my father and acted like I didn't care about having a father figure in my life, it was such a big worry in my head when I was a child. Still now, it is. I was created with a man. Why must I be raised without my creator? My perfect mother never mentioned much about him.

I was constantly reminded of how it would be like if I had my father around. Waiting for the school bus outside with my mother, I often saw children like me hand in hand with their fathers in the chilly morning days, laughing, happy, calling their dads "Daddy." That was something I often imagined myself doing, having him carrying me and telling me how proud he was to have me as his child. I spent most of my life imagining things that I will never experience and things that will never be. Even now as my soul wanders I still picture the things I never got to do with my mother and father as a family.

As my bones clinched together, I quickly pictured my father, whom I didn't know, teaching me how to ride a bicycle, taking me to school, and, my favorite, doing what fathers do—telling me how to avoid vagabonds. I was good at creating a picture-perfect father who may not even know I exist. When it came to drawing a perfect picture of my father and I, something always goes wrong to disrupt the image. If it wasn't the cops arresting him, it was him fading away from me as things got happier. I never understood the meaning behind that. There was always something else coming in between us. Maybe the reason this happens was 'cause I never really met him in person, and my fantasies were not going to let me feel the sensation of what wasn't real. It would not let me feel the complete feeling of being wholesome.

My mother spoke seldom of my father. I can only remember two times that she had briefly said something about him. They were not good things. It was twice during her crack moment; she had looked at me and said, "Your father is the reason I'm in this mess." Again, one time she was walking with me to the bus stop, and she quickly mumbled to herself, "I hate your father," as she looked over and saw a boy being carried by his father to the bus stop. She and I didn't spend many years together, but reminiscing back, we had so much in common. We despise men.

Sharp pain piercing through the edges of what's left of me, I could no longer endure the pain of being HIV positive. Sleepless in the middle of the night, my body was being persecuted by electric shocks. Taser, that's how it felt to me. This was the year for me thinking to myself. I wasn't going to see my eighteenth birthday in my deteriorating form. I began to physically feel it; my every move was alerting me. My zombie form had begun to take its place. Nervous and out of my comfort zone, I begged Carole if we could go see my doctor one last time, knowing he could potentially have us banned from the hospital, emulating what the judge did to us. I only had two choices: either end my meaningless life or the doctor can find his heart and offer me treatment. I haven't gone since he discovered that I was positive; he said there was no point in coming back for checkups. I got discovered too late; the disease had already made its way to my organs. There was nothing he could do to help me, except send me home, according to him. He sent me home with a couple of medications that I could no longer afford. I thought maybe if he saw me then he'd have some sort of sympathy to help me out, a change of heart. I was hoping he could give me some gratis medication with his newfound heart. People can change if they allow themselves to, I learned that. We had nothing to lose but a lifeless body. She agreed to come with me. She wanted to see me get better. Nothing she did for me worked anymore. I couldn't even walk myself to the car. Struggling to walk in my form, I was already a goner. I was trying hard to save myself. Naïve and lifeless, I didn't want to die. When my mother died, she left something to resurrect her, and that was me. For as long as I was alive, she herself was alive. I had my mother to fight for. I wouldn't let death take me away that easily.

Busting into the doctor's office, I saw a reflection of myself again. I've been trying hard to avoid seeing any mirror. This "me" caught me off guard; it was not the reflection I've been wanting to see. As I saw myself I quickly turned my head the other direction.

The doctor was utterly surprised, looking at our faces in his office once again when he had explained clearly before—no money, no care. He might as well have that statement written on the walls of the hospital. That statement was clearly clarified. We were wasting our time according to him, and according to us it was a time we were willing to waste. My lifeless body depended on him.

"What are you doing here? If you're here you must have the money."

"We don't! She's going to die, Doctor. Can you live with the fact that you could have done something to save her? If you can, we'll leave here, never to bother you again," Carole says to Dr. Jean.

"Good God, Jasmine, you're not the girl I saw five months ago. The disease must be spreading faster through your system," Dr. Jean said.

"We need your help, Doctor. I have no money to buy her the medications. The orphanage will no longer provide for her."

"Have you fought the court?" Dr. Jean asked.

"We tried, but they said that she was not their problem anymore because she's almost eighteen. They even had their security running us out of the court," Carole explained to the doctor.

"Here, have her lay here. Jasmine, can you hear me?" Dr. Jean said as he checked my vision.

I lay in his office chair while he takes his stethoscope to check my breathing. My breathing was shallower than usual. My oxygen level was only 60 percent high when it should have been above 100. The thing that kept my lifeless body alive was the low heartbeat that was pounding vaguely on the left side of my chest. It was going to stop soon though, soon enough it would. My blood pressure was below average. This didn't surprise me. Nothing in my body had the ability to function accordingly. With no insurance or money, there was nothing he could for me. The only thing I could do was lie in that hospital bed and wait for him to call his guards on us like the judge did. In this cramped

hospital bed I was either going to die or fight it with the help of
Dr. Jean. If the authorities saw the shape I was in and didn't offer
their kindness, what made me think a low-budget hospital would?
My hope was as shallow as my breathing. Lying in that bed I was
afraid of having Carole carry me back to the orphanage empty-
handed. I was afraid death was going to win. I couldn't let it win.
I didn't want it to.

"I'm surprised you're still alive. I'm not supposed to be doing
this without your health insurance information. If I get caught
I could lose my job. But I'm going to see if I can sneak in some
blood work for you," said Dr. Jean.

"Yeah, I'm not even sure she's fifty pounds," said Carole.

"Come with me, Carole, I want you to guide this door. If
anyone finds that she's here without any proper documents, I
could lose my job, and we both know for her sake we can't have
that," Dr. Jean said to Carole nervously.

"Oh thank you, Doctor. God will bless your soul," said
Carole.

"I hope so. Stay here. Don't let anyone come through that
door, you hear me, no one," Dr. Jean replied to Carole.

"Another thing—I can't guarantee you aid. Now again you
don't have any money. Doing this blood test will only allow me to
find out the degree of this," Dr. Jean said to Carole while he put
both his hands in his white jacket of shame—that's what I called
that jacket. It was good for nothing, only to bring hopes down.

"That's it! She should stay here overnight. She's too ill to go
back to that orphanage. Mr. Nelson doesn't want anything to do
with her. He won't spend a dime out of his pocket to help this
child. What's the point of doing this if you're not offering her
treatment? You couldn't possibly give this poor girl more bad
news than you've already done."

"Just stay here." He shut the door and ran down the corridor.

While Carole tried to convince the doctor that he was my last
chance, there I was hearing every bit of their conversation, but
I couldn't open my mouth to have a say. I lay there, constricting
my body to reduce the constant pain flowing through every inch

of it all. Standing at the door, Carole was concerned about my repeated grunts. She left guarding the door and came to comfort me. She held my hand and told me that I was going to be okay. She was very helpful, choosing the proper words to let me know things will get better when I already knew the truth; things will never get better. Her words of wisdom comforted me, gave me some sort of hope. She and I both knew that "I'm going to be okay" was not written in the books for me.

There was no chance that I was going to get out of the hospital feeling okay; "better" didn't apply to me. It never did. They were the lies that I wanted to hear. These words were mocking me. The one thing that could have miraculously made me feel okay was God, and that was not something I believed in. Carole was a strong believer in God. She had faith that I was going to come out of this. I did come out of it all right—dead, leaving nothing behind for the world to remember me by, only the trace that I was a prostitute who died from HIV. Praying was what she had come to know after her herbal medicines ran its course and my prescribed medications could no longer be refilled. No matter how hard she prayed at my hospital bed or at home, no matter how many scriptures she had read from the Bible before my bedtime, none of it helped. I'd get so frustrated hearing her praying out loud with her hands in my head like she was going to cast a demon out of me. HIV was the demon in me that prayers couldn't cast out. The only thing that made me feel less pain was the medications, and I was in dire need of them. If God does exist, he knows my pain in the flesh or in the soul. He ignored it all.

Leaving the door unguarded, a nurse passed by the room and saw that Carole and I were unattended by a doctor or a nurse. She walked in and asked us if a nurse had come in already to document my presence. "Excuse me, have you paid already to be in here?" said the nurse standing by the door.

Carole, nervous of being exposed, said in reply to the nurse, "Um . . . um, no, were waiting for a nurse." The nurse appeared extremely curious; no answers were good enough. "Why is she laying in this bed? She can't be in here if she hasn't been documented yet. This isn't your house, ma'am," she said.

I made an attempt to get off the bed but couldn't. I found myself plunging right back to the cramped bed. "Can you please help your child up, and you people need to wait outside." Where was this nurse coming from, talking to us the way she was? Because she was wearing a uniform, she was better than Carole and I. I admit, Carole and I, we were not in our best clothing. Yes, Carole's skirt may have had two gaps in it, and I may have smelled funny. We may have dressed poorly, but this was not a reason to be spoken down to by this nurse. Where does she get off calling us "you people." That uniform may have given her too much power.

"Can't you see she can't walk? She can't stand up on her own. We've been waiting here on you. Don't talk to us like we owe you. She's not going anywhere. Now why don't you do your job and get the documents. Run along now, like the little measles that you are," Carole said defensively.

"I'll be right back."

As the nurse walked out the door, Carole lifted me up to her back, rushing to get out of the hospital before the nurse returned with the forms. She made an effort to get me walking. I felt paralyzed; my body was numb in every aspect. She picked me up and carried me. By the time she opened the door the nurse was already on her way back to the room with the forms in her hands.

"Where are you guys going?" the nurse asked.

"Uh . . . uh . . . uh . . . she needs to use the bathroom. Is she not to use that too?"

"I've retrieved the forms. Ma'am, you can't carry her like this. You need a wheelchair."

The nurse called one of his assistants to bring a wheelchair out. "Jacque, bring this lady a wheelchair, will you?" she yelled out while snapping her fingers against the other.

I couldn't speak, I couldn't move, but somehow my heart had reached its capacity of beating. The beat of my heart started to drag just like the suspense of wanting to escape that nurse. I was nervous for Carole and I. Carole was so nervous she couldn't stop shaking. In her back, sweat was piercing through her shirt and onto my face. There was a lot at stake here. Carole could lose her job at the orphanage, and Dr. Jean could lose everything he'd work for if authorities got involved. That nurse was close to doing just that, calling authorities. With no hospital documents and no money, we were likely to find ourselves in jail. I already had a court order to stay out of the public eye, and here I was in hospital full of fortunate people waiting in line with their documents or checks ready to be signed.

"What's wrong with this young lady? She looks out of it. Take her back to the room. I'm going to ask you some questions, and then we can start putting her on antibiotics," says Nurse Marie. That was her name.

Nurse Marie told her assistant to run and get Dr. Jean. I was not a believer in God, but at that moment, I was praying unfaithfully to find a way to escape her. She was not leaving our side. I knew how much trouble we could get into if they find out that I was in the hospital "illegally." I knew for sure that I couldn't let Dr. Jean's name slip out of my mouth if I was forced to speak. There was too much to lose from this. He had a family to take care of. If they find out he already went to do blood work on me, that was enough for him to get his house and his job taken away from him, and he could go to prison if authorities find out he went this far. Authorities were very serious about their income at Judem Ville. If you had no money or no health insurance, it was a direct life sentence or death. It saves them the headaches of having to deal with the contaminated. Being poor was a disease to the authorities. They wouldn't offer you help even if their lives depended on it. People with no money were not human to them. Sometimes looking back it seems like we were stuck in the 1800s, our kind treating us like slaves, like nobodies, strictly because of the value of some papers. Orphans like me with no special gift get treated like peasants even more so if that orphan was dealing with a contagious disease like AIDS.

In the office, the nurse proceeded to ask us questions, or should I say Carole, 'cause being enervated didn't leave any room for that. In my mind I could speak, I could think, I had the answers to speak for myself, but getting the words out my mouth was a different story. My mouth felt frozen, like being in the North Pole, according to Daphne. Only Nurse Marie had the energy to keep us standing there speaking and talking.

"What's her full name? I need a name." She snaps her fingers again, demanding an immediate response. "My name is Nurse Marie, by the way."

"I need a name, ma'am!" Marie says. She was quick to say things right after the other, disabling us from gathering our thoughts before answering her questions.

"Uhh . . . Um, her name is Jasmine Pierce." In a nervous rush, Carole seemed to have forgotten my name suddenly.

"How old is she?" Marie asked.

"Seventeen."

"Are you her mother?"

"Uh . . . uh . . . um, I'm her orphan mother."

Orphan kids need help too. We're people too who needs health care like any other human being. Not to Marie though. To her being orphan was a problem.

The second Carole opened her mouth and said "orphan mother," Marie took a long pause and placed her writing hand around her waist and said, "Ahhh . . . this might be a problem in our hands." "Orphan" was another name for the people below the low class. It was a while until she proceeded to ask another question. Hearing that, I don't think she even wanted to ask the next question after hearing the contagious word "orphan." Following protocol, she continued after her long pause.

"Do you have health insurance?" Marie asked.

"No! She does not."

"How are you going to pay for her treatment? We can't move on with anything unless money or insurance is going to be exchanged here," Marie said in front her assistant Jacque, whom she was constantly yelling at.

"I'm going to pay with money," Carole says. She wasn't fooling me with that answer. She couldn't even find leftover food to feed herself after feeding us orphans. She goes to bed hungry, and here she was saying she's going to pay my hospital bill with money. What money? Whose money? Answers are left unknown.

Hearing that made me smile inside. The only thing I had was my name as far as I can recall. That was the only thing they couldn't control or take away from me. I'm sure if there were authorities for that, they'd have me nameless too. Anything they could shed off of me, they took.

"I just have to get to my car for my check," Carole replied to Nurse Marie.

"Oh no, we don't take checks. It's cash or insurance," Marie says.

"Okay, I'll be right back. I left my bag in the car. Can you walk now, Ja?" Carole asked me. What car? As far as I knew her wagon was parked in the back of the orphanage, rusting, catching feces from starving animals. Carrying me here to the hospital was a struggle. I'm sure if the car was really outside her blistered feet would be less swollen.

The nurse's voice rose after hearing that Carole was an orphan mom struggling to get by. She knew she didn't have money to pay for my medical bills. She works with orphans. That's the meaning of being an orphan. Misery finds you everywhere you turn. Carole didn't own a credit card or a checkbook or have cash. We lacked anything that had to do with money. That's why I was in the hospital pleading for pity. With the sweat falling off her face drop by drop, Carole could have honestly told her the truth about everything. Maybe she would reconsider her demeanor. Have a change of heart. It was a risk that couldn't be challenged though. Speaking for myself I was afraid of knowing her capabilities. She didn't look like the kind who had a heart. Her appearance changed quickly after she learned that we were "peasants." What could a frizzy-haired, bug-eyed nurse do for us anyway? She couldn't even hold herself to begin with, with her massive body frame. Her voice went from sounding like a girl to a man very quickly. If Carole didn't say that she could pay with cash, she would have instantly ordered us out of the hospital or call the authorities on us. She seemed ready to do it.

"She needs to stay here, ma'am," said Marie.

"Are you going to tell me what to do with my kid too? I'm taking her with me!" Carole responded to Marie.

"Oh don't let me stop you. While you go get your purse, I'm going to get Dr. Jean," she said as she moved aside away from Carole.

"Jasmine, Jasmine, can you hear me?" Carole said to me as she shook me from the wheelchair.

"I need your help right now. I need you to get up! And walk with me, Jasmine. Please get up," she begged of me.

I heard her. Grunting was all I could do in reply to her pleading. I took my hands and put them against the handles of the wheelchair to support myself. I found myself going right back into my broken self. "I need some water" is what I mumbled to Jacque, hoping he himself can leave my side.

"She needs some water. Don't just stand there," Carole repeated to Jacque.

"I'll be right back," Jacque replied.

Having both Nurse Marie and Jacque out of the hallway, Carole managed to sneak me out of the hospital before anyone returned. Holding me on her back, she rushed me out of the hospital. On the way back to the orphanage, I forced myself to tell Carole that I was done. I was tired of fighting something that will soon become nothing. I was tired of running from my future. I needed to rest and prepare myself for what's to come. That was the end of me; there was nothing left to fight for anyway. After my mother died nothing mattered much, only a slight idea of making her dreams come true. She wanted to see her only daughter grow up and make something of herself. My mission after learning she was never coming back was to fulfill her wishes. With degrading flesh and death following my every move, I was ready to raise my flag on following that dream; it was too heavy of a demand. I had now seen the light that dying would be the only way I could rest in mind, body, and soul. My age had determined my fate as well. If I was still fifteen or sixteen I would have gotten help from the authorities.

The only question left unanswered was, is there such a thing called heaven or hell? Which side was waiting for me? If there is, was it heaven? Something Carole spent nights teaching me about. Heaven is the place where all God's children go after death. Heaven is place free from all illness. If this place exist, that's the place I want to go, the place where everything is magnificent. I can't remember the last time I've done something remarkable for my kind, something good for them to remember me by. I will be remembered as the young prostitute who died of HIV. If Carole is right about hell, it was praising me, praising me for all my wrongdoings. Thinking back on the things I've done have led me to the direction of hell. I've done some pretty horrible things during my youth that I'm not proud of, things that would shut heavens' door for me. I was the cause of why numerous orphan moms had lost their jobs. Spending time with thieves only made me into one. I spent part of my short life doing the wrongs, unknowingly working to keep myself from entering heaven. When I should have been in school, I was hanging out with people that influenced me to do wrong. Stealing money from other orphan moms in order to click with a group of runaways who thought thieving was the way of life, that thieving was the way to make a living. Problem was it got us nowhere, only in deeper sinkholes; that way was no way to a promising future. Stealing clothing from people who were trying to provide an afternoon meal for their starving kids, people who struggled to make a living, I worked on making their lives uneasy. All the crimes committed in the past by my own hands have directed me to one path, a path that would send me down below. Prayers aren't going to help me now as my flesh leaves its soul. Waiting, and wondering is now what's left to do.

It was determined that hell was waiting for me; the things that I have done during my youth were acceptable down below.

It is a matter of time now that they come for me if it does exist. It is out of my hands.

Upon arriving at the orphanage from the hospital, the phone rang. Carole lay me down on the couch and rushed to pick it up. It was Dr. Jean calling shockingly, explaining to Carole how he saw everything play out from another patient's room but didn't want to intervene to protect himself. On his way from my lab work he saw Marie, and knowing how she is, he hid himself from us. He proceeded to tell her that he had jeopardized his career for me and that it could never happen again. If it were to happen next time, he would get caught. In this town people had many reason to be so protective of their jobs. Finding a job is a miracle for us, and because hunger was all around the town, it was understood clearly why everyone seemed to want to shelter their belongings so much.

"I'm very sorry that I could not help your child. I wish that there was something I could do. My job was at stake."

"At least you tried. Some people don't even make the attempt."

"With that said, I have very bad news for Jasmine. The disease has moved to the AIDS stage. It looks like it's spreading faster than I have predicted last time I saw her."

"Okay, my question is what can you do for her at this moment while she's still here with us?" Carole asked of the doctor.

"I can't do anything except pray for her. If there is a God up there, now is the time to pray," Dr. Jean replied.

"All I have been doing is praying. I have prayed countlessly, hoping for a miracle. When will God answers my prayers, Doc? He sent us to you for a reason," Carole said over the phone to Dr. Jean, pleading for him to help us out.

"The only thing I could do to buy her some time is send her over at Lhopitale pour la Maladie if she had money or health insurance, which we both know she does not have. If she did we wouldn't be having this conversation right now."

"We both know that. Even if I took extra shifts at the farm I wouldn't be able to pay for those treatments," Carole replied.

"I can't fathom why this happened to her. She's so young," said the doctor.

"What can I do to help her for the time being?" Carole says eagerly.

"Nothing. Right now, all of her major organs are failing to maintain her homeostasis. Her kidney has given up, she needs a new liver, and without money we can't put her on the list. Her liver is completely dysfunctional. I'm surprised she's still breathing."

"Can I give her mine?" Carole asked the doctor.

"No, you can't, Carole. What? You're going to give her your liver for a minute? She's dying, Carole. It's a matter of time now. What about you?"

"I've lived my life already. Now it's Jasmine's turn."

"She has AIDS, and her major organs are failing. The liver is not the only thing that needs to be replaced. First of all even if you could give her yours, we don't even know if it would work. You need to have the same blood type as her. And I couldn't live with myself if I let you do that anyway, give your liver away to someone whose running out of time?" the doctor said to Carole over the phone.

"So there is no other option?"

"None I'm saying to you. When can I meet you? I took some medications at the hospital for her. These medications will not do much for her, but they will ease the pain. I took a month and half's worth of medications. Hope she still lives till then. Let me warn you though, supervise her when she takes them. They can get radically addictive."

"Thank you so much, Doctor. I don't know how to thank you enough! You are a good man after all."

"Now hurry up before I change my mind. Meet me behind the hospital," says Dr. Jean.

"I'm on my way."

With a month's supply of medication, a newfound love arrived. The pills became both my friend and my enemy. When it was not needed to take them, I took them, filling a void of anger. Painless and alive, I secretly felt like I was on top of the world. Going to school, I felt hydrated and untouchable. The pills did everything except for the way the kids were treating me at school. That didn't seem to change or wasn't going to change anytime soon. They had already made up their minds about me and that was final. After lending Mark my only pencil in art class, I've come to the realization that no matter what is done to assure the needs of my fellow classmates, they will never be happy or even consider me as a friend.

For every emotional and physical pain purging through the core of my brain, I took a pill to help me cope with the idea that I, Jasmine Pierce, will always be Jasmine Pierce, the lonesome orphan girl whose dreams have been crushed right in front of her eyes. On a regular weekend twenty pills were being consumed; it was only twenty because being seen by the public eye was unavoidable. When I'm hidden from the public eye I'm no longer a target for people. I refused to go out on the weekends. The only type of activities I can remember doing while alive was going to school and skipping school to relax under Harmony's branch. On school days, the pills became my breakfast, lunch, and dinner. They were a way to get rid the anxiety of being manipulated by peers who shared the same environment as I.

The more golden Daphne's hair began to look, the more she began to disappear, like me. The more pills my stomach digested, the more courage and confidence I began to gain with the people in English class. The poorer she got, the more her fashion sense got ignored. In French class I can remember sitting in front of her, admiring and drooling over her styles, wishing to be in her shoes. I once wanted to be just like her. Not anymore though. Now I find myself loving my chosen path. I fly beneath the blue skies, not regretting being Jasmine Pierce, daughter of Elizabeth Pierce. I carry that name with pride and confidence.

Daphne now wears the same outfit twice in one week. The limo no longer brings her to school. Her mom is now her chauffeur or her two legs gracious God has given to her are now put to better use. I used to see her every morning being dropped off by her mother. Come French period, she was regularly absent. The time she did choose to come to class she defended me. She became a new person when everything fell for the worst with her family. Was the downfall of family what it takes for people to change around here? I kept thinking to myself, if Daphne can change herself to become a better person when will everyone else follow in her footsteps? She once ruled the school. If I was waiting for the downfall of every family to see a change among the students then I would never be alive to see it.

Feeling restless, scratchy, dehydrated, I went to French class, hoping that I could catch up with work from when my illness took a toll for the worst. Entering the classroom, one of my classmates, Charlene, decided to put me on the spotlight by yelling out loud, "You still exist." I stopped and look at her, mute for a few seconds. Nervously, I took my hood off my head and told her, "Up until right now, I didn't even know you existed." The class laughed and asked Charlene if she was going to let this homeless girl talk to her like that. Charlene was one of Daphne's former best friends. They used to do everything together at school—they sat next to each other in class, liked the same guy, and they were okay with crushing on the same guy. Breaking these two apart in class was a teacher's nightmare. When it came to group work, it was impossible for them to not be in the same group. As chatty as they were the professor once learned that separating them would be destruction to the other groups. When they weren't in the same group their chatty ways became louder, leaving the other kids to become chatty as well. It was always hard to learn something when they were separated. They carried their conversations around the room. They shared the same limo and same styles. At some point, Charlene began dressing the same way as her. Some days they would come to school dressing as if they were twins, and other days they'd have similar personalities. Now that Daphne can no longer afford the fancy clothes or have the fancy limo ride, she rides with Christina, the fake, the wannabe rich girl who lives in an orphanage kissing Mr. Nelson's ass. Everyone knew the only reason she befriended Daphne was because she was popular in school and she wasn't, because she was rich and she wasn't, and because Daphne was her ticket to America, according to the students in French class.

When Charlene made her comment to me, Daphne defended me in more ways possible. In the past she had asked some of the students to stop poking fun at me, but never has it been like this. As I stand near my desk, trying to gather my thoughts on what I was going to say to her in response to her humiliating statement in front of the class, Daphne quickly distracted the whole class by telling Charlene to shut up. Charlene remained silent for a moment, and then the whole class shouted out once again if she was going to let Daphne talk to her like that. Charlene, being the follower that she was, didn't want the class to think she was weak. "Why are you even here? Shouldn't you be in jail along with your thief of a father?" Charlene said to Daphne.

"Why, Charlene? As far as I'm concerned, you're the shoplifter, so you should be the one in jail," Daphne replied.

"I don't think you want me to go there. You're messing with the wrong person. Why don't I tell everyone what your father did and why you have been walking around the school looking like Ms. Homeless here, huh?" Charlene said, not wanting to hold anything back from her former BFF. Standing there, my body shook for both of them for having the courage to stand up in front of the whole class dishing their dirty laundries.

"You really think you're something, huh? My father, who you're calling a thief, has helped your family get back on their feet on numerous occasions, and now you want to sit here and pretend you're better than me now? How dare you!"

"Why don't you guys go on and finish your conversation outside. I'm trying to teach here. I'm tired of this. It's always the same thing with you guys," Professor Viviane said, yelling at the students. She herself was tired of the constant fights among her students. The class was turned into a drama class rather than French. Some of us weren't learning anything because we were too busy trying to keep up with the constant rumors and dramas.

Ignoring the teacher's remarks, Charlene and Daphne proceeded to go on at each other's throat as if they've been waiting for this day to lash out at one another. I was in the middle of something I wanted to be nowhere near. After the fight was over, were they going to come at me, blaming me for starting up their fire? Timidly I wanted their argument to end, giving me a reason to run away from it all. Far away to Harmony was where my mind was at while being in the center of their argument. Questions were running through my head left and right. I even thought maybe I could just walk out of French class, leaving them to finish their fight. I didn't want to be part of the reason their friendship worsened.

"For anyone who does not know what's going on here with Daphne's father, let me fill you in. Daphne's rich father"—she quoted with her fingers—"has been in jail for months now for stealing money from his investors. The judge gave him a thirty-year sentence for being a thief."

Charlene couldn't possibly see how evil she was to me at that moment. How can you betray someone in front of a crowd who's been such a support to your family? Daphne's friendship had no value now if she couldn't keep the limo rides, the shopping, and the monthly vacations going. As long as it continued she would be there for Daphne sucking every penny she got. Now that she has none of this wealth going on, Daphne to Charlene is nothing. You can never know if your friends are truly there for you or for your money. Charlene was a prime example of someone who can love you for the amount of dollars you had in your pocket. I felt sorry she was this way.

"First of all, Charlene, you don't know what you're talking about. You're a conniving liar and a user. Now that I'm broke you turn everyone against me. You and your family are the same way—a bunch of moochers sucking the blood out of my family. I've known you since pre-grade school. I thought you were my friend until I find out that you and both your parents were using my family's fortune," Daphne says.

"Fortune? Is that why you and your family are living on welfare? Is that why your house, your cars, your clothes are now possessed by the authorities?" Charlene said as she counted her fingers for everything that was taken away.

The whole class turned their attention to both Daphne and Charlene, wanting to know more. Professor Viviane took her chair and sat down and said, "Why don't I let you teach the class."

"Who d—"

Right after Daphne opened her mouth to speak, Charlene quickly said to her, "Shhh . . . you have nothing to else to say or nothing that I want."

Daphne ran out of the room bursting in tears. That moment reminded me of myself from when they used to run me out of the classroom. Sad and embarrassed I lifted up my head, took a deep breath, and said to Charlene, "What's in your mouth? It looks like you have herpes. Now Charlene I know you have said this is a cold sore, but if I were you, I would get it checked."

Ryan, who was sitting right next to her, got up and moved four desks away from Charlene shortly after hearing what I had to say, so did the boys who were sitting in front and in the back of her. With that said, she sat down quietly. Shaking, I had woken up and felt my adrenaline pumping. It felt good knowing that finally I had a voice. I wanted to keep going. I wanted to tell her off more. I wanted her to feel bad about running her mouth about Daphne the way she did. Charlene was not the only person I wanted to tell off while I had this bit of energy piercing through my blood. So many things were going on inside my head. I wanted to tell Iris to go fuck herself for tackling me down the stairs. I wanted to say something to each one of them for making my life a living hell. Something struck me. If I told them the things that I pictured in my head then what would that make me? It would make me just as mean and sick minded as them. I've had my share of being mean to people, and I was not about to go back on that path. Being mean and rebellious is what got me here in the first place. I was better off ending the day the way I did. Hopefully now they will think twice before talking bad about me, or they can forget I ever stand up for myself, which they did.

Soon after French class was over, the news of Daphne and her father was the top trending topic in the corridor. Everyone seems to have partnered up with someone to talk about what Charlene had decided to share with the class. Christina, who wanted to see Daphne fail from the beginning, was celebrating in the school cafeteria. She was high, and she's walking with a smile on her face, hearing other students downgrading her worst enemy. To Christina she saw Daphne's downfall as a triumph of her winning popularity in the school. After all she was dating her ex. Daring myself to walk the school cafeteria, fearless after calling Charlene off, she shoved me against the wall right in front of Christina. My food fell. They both laughed while I picked my food up as they walked away. Christina turned her head to the side and threw a fake smile that read, "I got you for screwing my plan up." Her smile was just as phony as she was anyway.

I can understand Charlene's bullying ways, but Christina, out of all people, I shouldn't be surprised of her actions; and she was still holding a grudge against me for ruining her chance of seeing her drug addict of a mother. I lived with her. I knew the kind of person she was and still remains to be. She is the kind of person who thinks her beauty will get her far in life. If Charlene really knew the Christina I know, I bet the circumstances would have been different. For all we know Christina could have been shoved up against the wall also by Charlene, the greedy girl who wants to get involved with anyone who she thinks might have money. We walked these walls with secrecy and tried hard to prove to people that we are the people we were pretending to be at school, that we hold nothing but the truth. Really? I see it the other way around, nothing but lies and tormentors. Christina held a secret, I held a secret, and our former popular girl at school got her secret exposed by her former BFF. We all held secrets that separated us from ourselves. We all tried hard to avoid the dislikes or the opinions of our peers that we might not agree with. Daphne's secret was out. Now everyone knew the truth of why her lifestyle has changed so drastically over a short period of time. In the corner, I had my speculations just like everyone else. We were a distance away from knowing the truth.

It's easier to lie than to tell the truth. The truth is what sets us free, but yet we choose to struggle with the idea of letting people get close to us for fear of getting hurt. The truth was, after Charlene unveiled Daphne's secret in front of everyone in class, let's just say I was not the only one secretly eating lunch or spending time in the bathroom during recess. While forcing myself to eat, I heard a cry coming from the next toilet. At first I wasn't sure who it was. Crying in the bathroom used to be me. Now that I've stopped, someone had kept the tradition going. The crying went for seconds, and then seconds turned into minutes. The closer I point my ears to the bathroom walls, the more I could identify the voice of that person. The person would stop crying, and shortly after I would hear sneezing, wheezing, coughing, and lots of nose blowing continuously. What had come to mind at first was maybe someone got dumped that day; a lot of that was going on around the school. Very often someone would go there freshening themselves up after being dumped, hoping no one will notice their fear of rejection. The crying coming from the next toilet over didn't sound like Daphne at all; her voice was not this sharp, like I heard at first. The person sounded like they were in deep pain, sort of like when I'm crying. I thought to myself could it be Daphne in there? Putting together how she ran from class sobbing I figured that was her in there, still grieving being outshined by Charlene. When the school bell rang, we both opened the door at the same time. When she saw me, she was surprised. She was sure that she was the only one there. As quiet as I was, it was very hard to tell if someone was using the toilet or not.

She quickly grabbed some paper towels to wipe her drenched eyes, trying to get herself together as fast as she could before anyone else sees her vulnerable. She asked me, "What are you doing here? Have you been listening to me this whole time?"

"Uh . . . uhmm no, why would I? It's none of my business."

"Don't be stupid. Everyone knows about me now because I was trying to defend you."

"I didn't put a gun over your head and tell you to protect me. I didn't need your help. I could have defended myself on my own. The problem here is you. I am not your enemy here, Daphne. Charlene is! Whatever else you have to say, take it up to her."

"I'm sorry, I just have so much going on right now, you know, and on top of that Charlene just made my day even worse. Running away from this town is the only way my mind will ease up," says Daphne with a short smile.

"Welcome to my boat," I said back to her.

"So what's your deal? All this time I haven't seen you eating lunch at the cafeteria. You've been eating lunch here. Isn't it gross? 'Cause I find it disgusting having your food mixed with the smell of this latrine," Daphne said to me.

In reply I told her, "At first it was, but I've gotten used to it. It's really not that bad. In here you get all the latest news about heartbreaks, who's hot right now, and who's not, etc."

"Well, I'm not so hot anymore in here. I bet you've heard a lot about that."

"Trust me, yes, I have." We both laughed.

"You want to get outta here? I have this cool spot that I discovered a while back while you were away for so long. I notice that. Just because I've never really spoken to you on a friend level, don't think I don't know when you're not around," she said to me.

"I thought you hated me. You used to make fun of me in class, Daphne. Don't think I have forgotten about that."

"Yes, I know, and you have every reason to hate me right now," Daphne said as she got closer to me.

"Since we're on this subject, you are an easy target for people to make fun of. You wear the same thing almost every day, you have this weird odor that pushes people away, and another thing—I know being skinny is the 'it' thing now but you have nothing. You're just skin and bones. You look very malnourished. It's unnatural. Are you suffering from cancer?" she asked. *I'm not*

*suffering from cancer. I'm suffering from HIV, the worse chronic disease
one can possibly die from,* is what I wanted to tell.

Here I am standing face-to-face with the person that first hurt
me when I entered the school. I knew Daphne was in no position
to criticize my appearance, honestly or not. In the bathroom I
saw a side of her that I would love to get to know, a side that I
wanted to be friends with. Besides, it was about time that I got a
buddy to have lunch with in the bathroom. Unpopular, she had
no friends and I had no friends, so it made perfect sense that we
did become good friends in the long run.

We waited long after the corridor of Judem Valley High
emptied out until we could finally sneak out of those moldy doors
that imprisoned us for so long. Who would have guessed I would
be skipping class with Daphne, the once spoiled rich girl from
out of town. Still to this day I remain surprised for the kind of
young lady she turned into. Halfway into school, we're walking
and sharing conversations never shared with anyone else. When
Christina decided to talk to me, it was easily noted that every
word coming out of her mouth was fake. If anyone couldn't see
that then they were a fool. I couldn't see it; therefore, I was a fool.
Knowing she was unreal and wanting a friend I fell for her plans.
With Daphne it was different. We were sharing smiles instead
of rules or regulations. Deep down inside I wished I knew this
Daphne long before. I didn't have much time on this planet to get
to know this Daphne. Walking and talking, I noticed we were
taking the same route I usually take to Harmony.

Every step we took was taking us in the direction of Harmony.
The "cool spot" she talked about was Harmony. In the distance
I saw my animal friends running toward us, even happier than
usual. There were more of them than I had encountered. Could
they have multiplied because of Daphne? In the beginning there
were ten of them altogether. Now there's an army, an army that
couldn't be counted by me. This place was the place. It left me
unsatisfied, knowing that Daphne and I may not be the only ones
who come to this place for a break from it all.

"This place has been my secret for quite some time now," Daphne said.

"This place is my secret. I've been coming here since the fourth week of my sixteenth birthday."

"Really!"

"I started coming here the first week I came to this school. Remember the day you threw that pen at me when I was writing on the board?"

"I don't remember a lot of things I did to you, but let's not go to bad memory lane." She did remember. I wouldn't want someone to refresh my memory if I knew of how evil I was too.

"I thought I was the only one who knew of this place," I said to her. "It looks undiscovered. Another thing—do you notice the animals can speak? Or is it just me pressing the bars?"

"Yeah! At first I thought I was going crazy, out of my mind. The more I continued to come here, the more I see their world as the real world and our world as the dream," Daphne replied.

Knowing that I had someone to share this exciting place with enlightened my heart. In some weird way it was an emotional cure as well. Knowing that I wasn't the only one who understood the animals had brought some comfort. At least I knew then I wasn't crazy about the abnormal activities happening under Harmony's branch. At that moment, I felt sad and happy. Sad because finally I had a friend my own age that I could share my thoughts with but according to Dr. Jean, in my calendar I had only two months left here on Earth. I was happy because I was no longer walking by myself to find rest under Harmony's branch.

For the next few weeks Daphne and I were friends. She may have not thought of me as her best friend, but I saw her as my best friend, my first real friend. We walked to school together, and we swapped lunch in the bathroom. In the beginning when people saw us walking and talking together at school, they stared at us. In class they threw paper balls at us, calling us names. If it was a while ago, I would care about being bullied by my peers. When she came into my life, we laughed at the jokes thrown at us instead. In French class I no longer sat in the front. I sat in the back with Daphne, my newfound friend. We worked in group class together. A group glass used to consist of only me and paper balls being thrown at me. Since she and I became friends, it became just the two of us, till the day I died in her presence. In my spirit I see her struggles, a girl with beauty and brains who sees she has nothing to offer the world. What used to be love turned into hate, hate strong enough for her to hurt herself in times of despair. Watching down below makes me realize why she was the one who became my friend when I needed one the most. I will never forget what she did for me. She was a person with a heart strong enough to raise a population on its feet, yet no one sees it but me.

To continue with the story, Daphne and I became inseparable while Christina despised that I had finally found a true friend in her worst enemy. We did everything together in school. When we were tired of being called a loser in the cafeteria, we'd find ourselves in the bathroom, where our friendship originated; instead of tears we shared laughter. Carole noticed a change in me; the sad face I carried with me for the past nine years since I've been removed from my mother's care became a smiley face. Her presence replaced the need for the pills. With not many left, the weeks flew by quick. With her being by my side, the pain was ignorable.

When we did decide to skip school, Harmony was the place we called home. In the pond where my mother appeared to me, I spoke to her of everything my mother and I talked about. She'd dip her feet in the pond while I bathed in it with my loving mother. In the pond I spoke to my mother of Daphne.

"I see you made a friend," my mother said.

"Yeah, she's my friend from school," I said back to her.

"I know that already. You don't even have to explain." That pond was the only place my imagination would let me see my mother. From what I've witnessed under those divine branches, I started to believe the beings had something to do with it. My mother was someone I wished to bring back from the afterlife.

"Who are you talking to? There's no one in the water, Jasmine." Daphne laughed. "You are as crazy as they say you are."

"Who are they?"

"People at school. They talk about you very unpleasantly," she said as if I didn't already know.

I dive to the shore of the pond and told her, "I'm talking to my mom."

"Your mom? There's no one in the water. Ha ha, you're funny."

"She's here! She's staring at you as we speak," I replied to her. She looked at me as if I was crazy. Why couldn't my imagination of my mother be true? If she could also understand the abnormal activities happening under Harmony's branch, why couldn't the fantasy of my mother be as real as us understanding the language of the animals? There wasn't a day I was at the pond that I didn't see the beautiful face of my mother telling me that everything was going to be okay.

"Let's head back to the school. My mom is picking me up soon. Do you want a ride to your house?" Daphne asked.

"No, I'm fine. My house is not too far from the school." I wasn't fine. My feet were killing me from walking back and forth. I wanted to say yes to that ride. It's been a while since I rested my feet. They began to swell just like Carole's feet. I trusted Daphne but not enough to let her and her mother drive me to an orphanage, an orphanage that was a whistle away from falling off its feet. It was no place for guests unless it was someone coming to take one of us away. Christina worked hard on keeping the truth from being told. Taking that ride from her could have jeopardized what she's been trying to prove to the school.

Getting back to the school, Daphne introduced me to her mother. "Hi, Mom, this is my friend Jasmine."

"Hi, Jasmine. I'm Judith. How come I've never met you before? Are you new to the school?"

I said no.

"Honey, I know all your friends. How come you never introduced Jasmine to me before?"

Daphne struggled to answer her mother. I rushed in and said, "That's because we just recently crossed paths."

"Mhm, if you don't mind me asking, are you all right? You don't look too well."

"I'm great. Why are you asking?" I asked her.

"I'm a retired nurse. Now I know illness when I see one. Aren't you hot wearing all these layers of clothes?"

"Mom, let's go! You're always trying to get inside people's heads. She's not one of your patients, for God's sake!"

"It's okay. She can ask questions if she wants to." It was not okay. I had no truthful answers to give her. She was right. Underneath those layers of garments was a sick child suffering from AIDS. My disfigured body couldn't hide itself from civilization any longer. Just a glance at it told the honest story of a sick child.

"Do you want a ride home?" Judith asked me.

"Mom, I have already asked her. She's fine. Now let's go!"

"All right! What's wrong with you today?" Judith said to Daphne.

"Nothing, I just want to go ho—" Then she stops, realizing there was no home to go to. Everything her father had was seized by the authorities. Charlene may have betrayed her at school, but she did speak of the truth. Based on the look on Christina's face, their life was over. There were no more vacations to America, no more bringing American fashion magazines to class, no more Charlene to mooch off of the belongings that she no longer had.

Driving away I overheard Judith asking about Charlene. Charlene found a new rich friend named Christina; that's where Charlene's mind was at. Charlene was at school calling her husband a thief, that's where she was. If I were Daphne I would probably choose not to tell my parents of the unpleasant conversations being said about my family, the unpleasant conversations that are now the reason behind the ruined reputation of her daughter. Staring at Daphne in the passenger seat, she was not happy. She was an emotional wreck fighting to keep herself intact just like I've tried to do the same under the layers and layers of clothing.

Spending time with Daphne as often as I was, I had plans to tell her the truth about myself, the truth about everything I knew of, including telling her of the real Christina. Christina often asked why I was hanging out with her so much. She gave me ultimatums to drop her as a friend, but I refused to. She had too much control over too many people. I refused to be one of those people. One day she barged into my room and pointed her fingers at my face and said, "I need you to stop talking to Daphne at school. You need to go back to being the lonely girl that people hate at school."

I told her, "Why you are inside my room? Aren't you afraid of getting AIDS? I'm contagious."

"I bet Daphne doesn't know what you're sick from. You haven't told her, have you?"

"Why are you so worried about what I tell her or not? She's not you. If anyone hasn't told you, let me be the first one to tell you so. You're a user! You and Charlene should be sisters!"

"So now because you have one friend you have a backbone, huh? I will tell Mr. Nelson that Carole has been using our money to feed your contagious ass."

"Is that so? Go ahead, go! And I will tell the whole school you're not this little rich girl that you pretend to be."

"Let me tell you this. I can assure you Daphne will want nothing to do with you once she finds out that you're dying from HIV. Prostitute!"

"And you think Charlene will want to be your friend once she finds out you're an orphan? Wait till she finds out you sleep in an orphanage of twelve. She'll turn against you just like she did to Daphne. You're nothing without your lies, Christina, let me assure you of that!"

Was I about to lose the only friend that I've just made? What if she is right? What if she doesn't want to be my friend after knowing the truth? Christina was manipulative. She could twist the truth and tell everyone the same thing the judge told the court—I was a young prostitute dying from AIDS. She's the kind of person who would do anything to take away any chance I had of being happy.

"Don't think I won't tell the school that you're running around spreading a disease. What you have on me is nothing compared to what I have on you," Christina said to me.

I got off from the bed and closer to her. "Don't cross me!"

"You have a backbone now! I will show you what having a backbone really means. Watch me," said Christina, walking away from me. I shut my door, worrying about what she might do. She is capable of lots of things. She could get me kicked out of the orphanage as quickly as she wanted to. All she had to do is give Mr. Nelson a call. She has more power over me now and she's proud of it. I could take a pill to make all of this go away, but I'd wake up in the morning facing reality.

Christina had been another reason why this man wouldn't stop haunting me. Every time the arguments get intense between Christina and I, the flashbacks too get intense. Christina feeds my flashbacks and the nightmares. Forcing myself to close my eyes, I felt a man grabbing me with force. I wake up. Nothing. I close my eyes again, and the man comes back. The faceless man finds his way back inside my loaded head. Provoked from sleeping in the dark I find my way to the kitchen, where Carole arranges her bed. I woke her up and said to her, "Please make this man go away."

She turned on her gas lamp and walked me out of the kitchen. "What man, honey?"

"The man in my room. He won't stop grabbing me," I replied to her.

"Come with me. No one is in your room, Jasmine," she says.

"Yes, there is. I saw him. The faceless man. He's hiding from you. If I close my eyes, he will reappear again."

"Are those nightmares coming back again? See, I checked. There's no one in here. Now you say when you take the pills, you sleep well, right?"

"Yes."

"Take a couple of them. It's really late. Now where's that bag?" My pills were done. I had nothing left to rid my untold wound. I swallowed them like food. Doesn't she think if I had more I wouldn't be waking her in the middle of the night? I've been hiding the fact that they've been gone now for weeks.

"Jasmine, why is this bag empty? Don't tell me those pills are done already? What have you done, Jasmine!" she screamed at me.

"Nothing."

"I saw the quantity of what Dr. Jean gave you. They cannot possibly be done already." With nothing to report, I knew of my shame. I laid there in silence with the sheets covering my head.

"Answer me, Jasmine! Answer me, damn it!" Carole yelled out loud. "Did you relocate them somewhere else?" she says as she turns the cramped room upside down. She checked the window, threw my clothes off the closets, checked under the bed. She checked everywhere there was to check in that little room, only to find empty bottles. I could have easily told her the pills were gone, done. I consumed it all is what I should have told her. Instead I let her turn the room upside down, looking for an answer that wasn't there.

To make the situation worse, I told her, "Can I sleep with you?"

"No, Jasmine, you're not sleeping with me! How can you do something so selfish? We have gone through so much to get those pills. My feet are still swollen from that horrible day I had trying to make sure you survive longer."

Yes, selfishly I wasted the pills. Even when I didn't need to take a pill, I took one, hoping my problems would go away. Selfishly I took pills to skip my flashbacks, my nightmares, the faceless man who wouldn't leave me alone when I closed my eyes. Selfishly I didn't think about the next day or the next month or saving those pills for when it's really needed. "You are on your own, Jasmine. I'm not going to kill myself over someone who only thinks of herself," Carole says.

I screamed, "I'm sorry!"

She left the room upset, furious, thinking wrong of me. She called me selfish; "selfish" was the word used to describe

Christina. Now I was a selfish being according to Carole. How can I let myself get this far? The doctor warned me of the pills, but I chose not to listen. She trusted me. I lost her trust. Struggling to keep my eyes open from that dark man, I thought what I did was selfish. We were now left to beg again because of me. Sooner or later the pills would reach its limits, but it wouldn't be because of my own selfish needs to prevent darkness or to ignore my fate; in actuality it'd be because I cherished each pill like it was the last one.

In darkness I see nothing but the man that raped me years ago. Without the pills I see nothing but the man that took my childhood away from me. Suffering from the things that haunted me, I find myself planning ways to get those medications back. If I get them back I could do things differently now, wisely, and show Carole that I was not selfish. The idea of stealing comes into my mind, stealing from Christina that was. I found where she kept her stash. She had enough for two bottles of those pain killers. Contemplating is as far as I could go. Going back to my old self was not a good idea. Stealing got me in many troubles. I had enough troubles as it is to open the door for new ones. I could go back to that hospital and plead for more pills. The refills date was nowhere near. I abused those pills like no other, how could I go back asking for more? Dr. Jean went through a lot of trouble to get me those pills, and I chose to eat them like food.

A disappointment to Carole, she herself started avoiding me at the house. She went back to working at the farm, working more hours than ever. When she comes back to the orphanage, she was too tired to even fix us dinner. Bread and sweetened water became our nightly meal. Ryan, who used to speak a few words to me, speaks none anymore. Dying of hunger, I would wait till everyone was sleeping and steal some bread off the table to feed my troubled stomach. I'd eat the bread outside because I knew I was going regurgitate it shortly after. Some nights Carole hears me, my dying moans, but she ignores them. I wasn't mad at her for ignoring me like everyone else.

Trying to avoiding being seen as ill at the school premises, I kept the layers heavier on my back. Christina wasn't at school that day. This was the first time in a long time Christina was absent from school. Where was she? That same morning she taunted me with her new outfit. It's not like her to skip school. The closest she came to missing school was when she wanted to find her mother. I spent the whole day in school, and Christina was nowhere in sight. There were no rumors at the orphanage about Christina going anywhere. Daphne wasn't in school either that day. The school's biggest people were missing. For Daphne's absence, I wasn't surprise. There are times she's weeks absent from school, and since the tragedy that hit her family, she was frequently absent. Christina, on the other hand, had very little reason to be missing school. Everyone aside from Daphne and I worshipped her.

Spending my recess in the bathroom, they were talking about her being absent from school. People missed her and hoped that she was okay. People also had speculations she wasn't the kind of person she was pretending to be. Shocking, I find that, and I meant that sarcastically. Charlene was in the bathroom talking to one of her friends who was one of her followers. She had a name. Her name was Julmina Bastien, but I called her the "follower" of Charlene. She did everything Charlene asked of her, just like Charlene did everything Christina asked. I overheard Julmina saying, "I heard some talks around that Christina lives at the Nelson orphanage."

"Well, that's a lie because Christina showed me her house weeks ago," Charlene said.

"Where does she live?" Julmina asked her.

"You know that big house behind the hospital for the sick?"

"Yeah, I've seen it," Julmina replied.

"Well, that's where she lives. Her parents are loaded."

"Have you been inside?"

"No, but she says when she has time she'll take me for a tour."

"Can I come with you when she does?"

"I'll think about," she said to Julmina as she took her lipstick from her hand.

"Do you ever think maybe she's lying to you?"

"Have I hung out with people who weren't meaningful to society? Take Daphne, for example. You're the only exception, Julmina, because you do everything I ask you to do."

"I'm only saying, Charlene. And where is she today?"

"I know where she is. She's packing for America. That's why she's not here today. She's going to America for the weekend. If you were her friend, you would know that. She's says she's going to take me there someday, and if you're good enough, you can come too."

Ha ha ha. Hearing Christina lived in a big mansion and was spending her weekend in America gave me the sudden rush to laugh. She was more comical than I thought. That big mansion Christina had those girls thinking she lived in, I knew who it belonged to. It was the mansion of Ryan's friend Emanuel. His parents lived in that mansion. I can see why she told them that mansion belonged to her. That mansion was a golden fit for the mentality of someone like Christina. That mansion was surrounded by guards who wore special uniforms. It has fences that are code activated. This mansion was a mansion fit for a movie star, but according to Christina this was her mansion, where she lives in happily ever after. She was a bigger liar than I thought too, very convincing. If I didn't live with her at the Nelson orphanage, even I would believe she lived like a princess.

Heading back to the orphanage, it hits me again that I was soon a goner. I have nothing left. As the pain becomes more intrusive, the more I believe it was only a matter of time before Carole finds me in bed breathless, cold, ready to be put in a hole where I can now be identified as simply a number. When I walk alone my mind gets me thinking a lot about myself and my disease. The pain got me worried of my time here on Earth. I got to the orphanage, and Christina wasn't there. Everyone was at the house but Christina. Mr. Nelson shouted, "Hey you, have you seen Christina?"

I lift up my hood and answered him timidly. "No, I have not seen her. She wasn't at school today."

That was a question I spent the entire day asking myself. "Where was Christina?" It wasn't like her to disappear. If she's going anywhere she hints around that she was going somewhere. I had an idea of where she could be though. It rings in my head that she went out of her way to find her mother alone.

"Did she tell you she was going somewhere?" Carole asked me.

"She did say she wanted to find her mother," I told Carole.

"Find her mother? Her mother died a few years ago. What is she talking about finding her mother? She never says anything about finding her mother to me," Mr. Nelson added.

"Let's go search in her room. Maybe there's something there that will tell us of her whereabouts," Mr. Nelson says.

Mr. Nelson was worried. Sweat was dropping off his face like droplets of rain, acting like he had just lost a child. He ran into her room with Carole following him. I also followed them to find a clue that will lead us to her. If anyone knew where she was, it was I. There was one place she spoke about frequently, and that was the place she thought her mother was. "I can't lose her. I can't lose her," Mr. Nelson repeats.

"We'll find her, I promise you that," Carole says to Nelson.

"This is all your fault, you know. If you were doing your job like you were supposed to she wouldn't be missing." Mr. Nelson was good at blaming people for his problems.

"I found something," I said to them. Under her bed lie the directions of her perfect plan to reach her mother. It was the same plan we had contemplated on a while back. Her directions couldn't be any more conclusive. It had the time and date of when she was going to get there. Mr. Nelson grabbed the paper out of my hand and said, "I know where that is. I know exactly where that is! Let's go!"

Carole grabbed her purse and ran to Mr. Nelson's car. "You kids stay here and behave. We're going to go find Christina and bring her home, you hear me. Everything will be fine."

"Can I come with you and Mr. Nelson? I can help you find her," I asked Carole.

"Okay, come on."

Getting ready to get inside Mr. Nelson's car, he asked, "Where is she going?"

"She's' coming with us. She knows Christina more than any of us. They go to the same school, Mr. Nelson."

"All right, get in and don't touch anything," says Mr. Nelson.

"I won't."

It was six o'clock, and Christina was missing from the orphanage, adding more problems to the list.

In the car, Carole took the chance to speak to Mr. Nelson about many things. They talked as if I wasn't in the backseat listening, Christina was the topic. It wasn't about why we were searching for her. It was more about Mr. Nelson's feelings toward Christina. "Can I say something?" Carole asked.

"Of course," Mr. Nelson says.

"If this was Jasmine who had gone missing, I'm sure you wouldn't go through all this trouble to find her. Is there something you know that I don't know?" Carole says.

"Jasmine has a history of running away, Carole. Have you seen her profile?"

"It's not just that. I have seen how you give Christina special attention. She's the only one who gets spending money for herself at the house. Christina is the only person you see at the house, Mr. Nelson, and it's not fair to the other ones," Carole complained. Still ignoring my presence in the back passenger seat, they continued with their conversation. "I don't know how to speak of this Carole. I have done something relentless. If she finds out the truth of who I am, she will hate me."

"What truth?" says Carole.

"I promised myself I would never tell anyone of this, but it seems I may have no choice. I'm the reason why were in this situation right now. I'm the reason, and I don't blame her if she chooses to never speak to me again."

"What is it!" Carole asked eagerly.

Sitting in the back, listening to every bit of their conversation, even I was eager to find why Mr. Nelson was blaming himself for the disappearance of Christina. I wanted to understand why he treated Christina differently than all of us. I sat in the back, quietly waiting for Mr. Nelson to spill out this secret he's been holding from the orphanage.

"Stephanie Precilien, Christina's mother, and I used to have relations." No wonder she was getting special privileges. He couldn't possibly like Christina sexually. At first my assumption was he had feelings for her, after all she was a beautiful girl with an ugly hear. Again beauty mattered in that little town of mine. No one cared for age. I didn't come close to thinking about Mr. Nelson having relations with Christina's mother. This was news to me. I'm sure Christina did not know any of this.

"What! I have known you for decades now. How have you not told me this? I know everything about these kids. Don't you think that's something you should have told me?" Carole said to Mr. Nelson.

"That's not all. I left her mother because I couldn't handle her habits any longer. Leaving her was the biggest mistake I have ever made. Her drug habits got severe after I left her. I moved to this town hoping to forget about her, which I did while managing these kids."

"Is that the reason you pay more attention to Christina?"

"Let me continue. Before she died, she left me a letter telling me that she was pregnant. She wrote in the letter that I had a beautiful baby girl named Christina Precilien. I was the father."

"What? No, there's no way."

"Well, that's what I thought. I did a DNA test and the test came out that I am really her father."

"How long have you known this?" said Carole.

Sitting in the back, I am traumatized by what I have just heard. Turns out Mr. Nelson was also carrying a secret, a secret that either can change Christina for the best or for the worst. If this was me, this news would not sit with me well. To have my father watch me live in a cramped, overcrowded house and keep this secret from me, this would leave me infuriated.

"I have known this for seven years now."

"I am speechless. I really don't know what to say, Mr. Nelson. I thought I knew you, but I was wrong."

She wasn't the only one speechless. My jaw dropped upon hearing the news.

"Well, here we are!" Mr. Nelson said, turning the ignition of the car off. He turned around and said to me, "I know you heard everything I have told Carole. I need you to keep your mouth shut. Understand?"

"Yes." Oh trust me, I don't think I would want Christina exploding on me when she hears this. *She's all yours*, I said to myself.

"You can't keep this from her, Mr. Nelson. It's wrong! She deserves to know the truth," Carole replied.

"I will tell her when the time is right. Right now is not the right time. Her safety is all I'm worried about this instance."

Oh he had more than that to worry about. I was 100 percent sure Christina was in that little clinic. According to her this was the place where her mother spends her drug-free life at. Here I am again feeling sorry for her. Poor thing had a lot on her plate, a dead mother and a sixty-year-old man who was keeping a big secret from her. Her rich made-up life couldn't get any more bad news. Here she was telling people at school she lived in a big gold mansion and planning a trip to America; behind closed doors the people that were close to her abandoned her.

Upon entering the clinic, Christina was in tears, telling the news of her dead mother as if we didn't already know or as if her father, Mr. Nelson, didn't already know way before standing right beside Carole. I saw a side of Christina that I would love for people at school to see, a side that shows the vulnerability of imperfection. See that side that was human. For every drop shed, there was a little girl inside Christina dying to have a normal life.

"Mr. Nelson, I'm sorry I didn't tell you I came for my mom," she said while wiping her nose.

"It's okay, Christina, it's okay," Mr. Nelson said, taking a handkerchief from his pocket to wipe Christina's tears. It was beautiful. It was a moment beyond imaginable, a moment that I have often created with my imaginary father. That moment was even better than my fantasies, watching the two comforting one another. He hugged her and looked into her eyes and said, "I'm here for you. I promise. I will never leave you again. Everything will be okay. You believe me." I wasn't Christina, but I myself felt that warmth coming from Mr. Nelson. Selfishly I pictured myself being in her place at that exact moment.

"She's dead, Carole, and I never got to see her."

"I know, honey, I know."

"No, you don't know, Carole. All my life I've been planning on this day. It finally arrives, and now they're telling me she's dead! This is not fair!" Christina screamed.

"Mr. Nelson, can you please take me home?"

"Anything for you, sweetie."

"What is she doing here?"

"Who?"

"Jasmine."

"Oh she wanted to help find you."

"Why does she care?"

"She was worried about you. Everyone at the orphanage is."

On my way back to the orphanage, I couldn't stop thinking about being in the presence of Christina's father. I couldn't fathom that all three of us sitting in the car in silence knew who her father was while she sits there weeping over her dead mother, who has been dead for five years. I wondered how Mr. Nelson would tell Christina of this. Everyone remained silent until we reached our destination. Mr. Nelson left, saying to Christina, "I want you to know that I love you very much."

"Mr. Nelson, you're acting weird. In which way do you love me?"

"I love you like my daughter."

"Oh 'cause I'm only seventeen."

"Ha ha, you a funny girl, my child," said Mr. Nelson.

"Carole, can you take Jasmine with you? I need to talk to Christina. She'll be right in."

Wanting to know how Mr. Nelson was going to bring up the topic of how he's known Christina was his child and never did a thing about it was jumping through my brain. I was curious. I pretended I was going back in with Carole only to sneak back outside again; underneath the mango tree was where I hid myself to snoop in their father-daughter conversation.

Mr. Nelson asked Christina, "Will you hate me if I tell you a secret?"

"No! Not at all. I love hearing secrets." *Hearing this secret, I'm not sure you'll be too happy about it*, I thought.

"Pinky promise," Mr. Nelson says.

"Pinky promise." He reached in his pocket and handed money to Christina, thinking he could distract her from hating him after telling her of his secret. Christina loved money. That was something that tells me he was really her father. Mr. Nelson was also a sucker for money.

"I have wanted to tell only you this secret for a while now."

"Tell me then."

"I'm just afraid of how you might react after this. I don't want you to hate me."

"You're the only one who seems to really care about me here. You give me money. You buy me clothes, and on top of that, you make sure Carole takes good care of me. Now how can I dislike a man like you?"

"I'm glad you see me that way."

"Nothing could make me hate you."

"I'm your father!"

"What? Ha ha."

"I'm your father."

"Don't be stupid. No, you're not!"

"I'm not being stupid. I'm telling you the truth, Christina"

"You're Mr. Nelson, you can't be my father! My father wouldn't have the heart to leave me suffering in an orphanage."

"I'm sorry, Christina. I just found out five years ago, after your mother died."

"What! This is not happening. Please tell me this is only a dream, and I will wake up from this. Please, someone wake me up from this nightmare!" Christina says. You can never be woken up from the nightmares of actuality.

"How dare you! You are not my father! You will never be!"

Christina rushes back into the orphanage, shouting, "This is not happening! This is not happening!"

Mr. Nelson got in his car and drove away. What a coward he was. Who runs away when your daughter is at their worst time? Christina was his only kid as far as we knew. He probably doesn't know how to handle a narcissistic girl like Christina. Meanwhile, she's in the house demanding the truth from Carole. The truth her father had already said to her.

"Carole, please be honest with me. Have you known all this time too?"

"Know what?" Carole says, pretending she knows nothing about Mr. Nelson's escapade.

"Mr. Nelson just told me he was my father."

"Christina, no one knew of this but your father, Nelson. He is the one who kept the truth from you, not me, not anyone else here."

"How could he stand there and watch me suffer, knowing he was my father? I could never do that to my kid. He can go rot in hell for all I care. I don't care about them!"

"Christina, don't be mad. Instead be happy you know of your father. You're the only one in here who knows if their father breathes or is dead. Think of this as a blessing," Carole said to Christina.

"To hell with him! How can I think of this as a blessing, more like a curse. Just when I think finding out about my mother couldn't get any worse," Christina said as she ran in the direction of her room. It was no secret anymore. Everyone at the orphanage knew now why she was getting special treatment from Mr. Nelson. She can be mad at him for as long as she wanted to, but at the end of the day Christina was the daughter of Mr. Nelson, the owner of the orphanage where the twelve of us spent hating on one another.

Christina and I had our differences. She spent time at school making sure people prey on me. She had her problems and I had my problems. She knew well how to keep her trials hidden. At school she was the rich girl who just came back from America. She spent her days making people believe she lived in a golden mansion, something I couldn't do. No one would believe me if I told them I too was rich living in a mansion; my body would deceive me, which it has no problem doing. In the orphanage Christina was the definition of extreme anger. No one was allowed to speak a word to her, including Carole. According to her the orphanage was the devil while she ruled the school yard along with everyone in it.

Getting closer to my eighteenth birthday, I found myself leaving the house, walking to Harmony more often while Carole is away at the farm working her extra hours. After wasting the pills, I stopped complaining about the need for help to Carole. My condition was in my hands. It was my fault I was feeling the way I did. For the time left in the orphanage, my illness remained hiding from Mr. Nelson. I did everything on my own, proving to Carole I wasn't selfish. I washed my clothes even when I couldn't find the strength to. I'd wait till Carole goes in for work, sat out, and did everything that needed to be done, including doing the chores Carole had little time for.

It was about time now that death finds me. I was waiting, ready for heaven or the underworld. Most of the time I made my way to Harmony, where Daphne was bonding with the beings I found friendship with. Going there as often as I did, I was no longer a guest invading their territory. With their abnormal activities, I allowed myself to not question what is sane. In the beginning Daphne also experienced the same vision I experienced during the first few weeks I discovered Harmony. She kept nothing from me. Going there and seeing my friends interacting with her, my jealous instincts kicked in. I wanted to be the only that has this special gift.

"Where have you been, Jasmine? It seems you're always disappearing from school. You come and go. Sometimes you're absent for weeks. That will live a mark on your grade."

"Maybe I'm just not into school."

"Doing this is going to get you in that stadium, which is coming up soon." I'd be lucky if I get to graduate or have the strength to stand up in a line full of students rambling on about what's next for them. Humiliation was what kept me hiding under that oversized jacket, and making it to the stadium would do just that, get a bunch of inconsiderate students excited, shouting, "Go home!" I had absolutely no plan on graduating Valley High. I was very busy waiting for death.

"I know that's not the reason. We've been friends for quite some time now. I have told you everything about me, but yet you hide things from me."

"I'm not hiding anything from you."

"Jasmine, look at me. You can be honest with me. Our friends here have the ability to show us a vision of the truth." We leaned our body on the grass; the animals encircled us, allowing my flashbacks to be seen by Daphne.

"Hold my hand, Jasmine. They're trying to show us something. Close your eyes and I will close mine."

"You've been getting to know these guys, haven't you?"

"You have no idea what they're capable of. They can help you," Daphne said.

Closing my eyes, my flashbacks came back to me, forcing to get out of my head. Everything was backward. Everything seemed extreme, fast. I fought myself out of a combat. Moving my body, I can hear Daphne comforting me and telling me to let it be. I remained calm. I see the man catching me, but with strength I was able to fight my way out of a combat. I ran. The faceless man ran after me, catching me again before he could get the chance to have his way with me again. I shut my eyes deep, wishing for him to go away. By the time I opened my eyes, the man vanished.

How was this possible? My nightmares were never overturned. I opened my eyes, sweating, out of breath. With my eyes back to reality, the oasis was grassless, the branches that hung from the bridge were leafless, and the pond where I see my mother's face was without water. My animal friends were lying on the grass, unconscious. To prove I wasn't hallucinating, I asked Daphne, "Are you seeing what I'm seeing? What happened here?"

"You're pain is so strong that they take energy out of everything."

"What are you talking about?" I said to her.

"I know everything, Jasmine, you can trust me."

"I don't know what you're talking about."

"It's okay, Jasmine. It's okay to trust someone. I know what you're going through."

She handed me a piece of cloth. "What's this for?" I said.

"It's for your nose, it's bleeding."

Taking the cloth from her hands, I turned away. This wasn't the first time under Harmony that I've experience that. Last time I had a vision was when I fell from the stairs of doom. Upon my awakening, my nose also started bleeding. This was no coincidence. "Jasmine, look at me. I'm sorry, I really am."

"Sorry for what?" I asked her while holding my head up to block the blood from coming out of my nose.

"I saw your nightmares. I see what's keeping you awake every night. I know everything. I even saw that vision you just had."

"You do?" I asked her.

"And I'm not scared. That man who hurt you this much will pay," Daphne said.

"Your nose is bleeding too, Daphne," I told her.

"It's okay. I knew that was going to occur. I was expecting you today. Before you got here, they told me I would never understand your agony until I experienced it. I saw everything that you have been so afraid to speak of. There's nothing to be ashamed of, Jasmine. You didn't wish this on yourself."

There were a lot of things I didn't wish on myself, including being below poor that I can't even afford to get myself treated. My nose continued to bleed. I looked around, and the animals were still lying on the ground, unconscious. "Are they dead?" I asked Daphne, who appeared to know more of the beings than I. I was the first to discover them, but yet what I knew of them was very little compared to the load Daphne knew.

"Nah. They're okay. Your visions weaken them. Once you're gone, they'll be fine. I'll walk you home."

"Okay, good, because I am restless. I can't walk alone," I replied.

"Can I tell you something?" Daphne asked.

"Sure. Remember the first day I came to Harmony with you and walked back to the school where my mother offered you a ride?"

"How can I possibly forget about that day? Your mom interrogated me."

"My mother likes to stick her nose on everybody's business. But she's my mom though. I love her." I wish I could say the same. My mother wasn't around for me to say that. I didn't even get a chance to tell her I love her. The only place I could say I loved her was in that pond that is now waterless. I don't even know if it's real or if it's the beings' way of comforting me because they know she's such a huge part of me that has died.

"Well, she thought you had cancer."

"What? No way!" I said trying to put up a straight face. The way her mother undressed me with her eyes, it was impossible for her to avoid making judgments. "Can you blame her though?" Daphne says.

"You're right. I can't blame her. She was not the only one thinking that way," I said, trying to put on a brave face. My head was spinning, thinking of a plan to get rid of her. I couldn't let her see that I lived at an orphanage, and what if Christina is home? I couldn't be the reason her secret was exposed. Christina had too much going on already. I couldn't afford her taking her anger out on me. She's known for that—taking her anger out on people. I've been a victim of those too often. She was my support for walking. Getting to a close distance to the orphanage, I told her to let go of me and that I could walk by myself from there. "I'm walking you all the way home, Jasmine. I'm not leaving you like this."

"Leaving me like what? I'm fine."

"You're not fine, Jasmine. Anyone can look at you and see the same thing I'm seeing—an ill young lady who needs help, a lot of it."

"No, it's okay, I'm fine!"

"I don't care what you say. I'm walking you home and that's final!" I had no control over her. Close to the orphanage there were two little pine houses next to it. Looking at the two from a distance the orphanage was more acceptable to be my home. These two little houses were made out of fresh logs covered by all types of leaves. Nicole's former friends lived next door. I could have easily chosen Nicole's friend's house to avoid her knowing that I lived at a foster home, comparing the pine houses to one another there was one problem, at the front of it wrote "Nelson's Orphanage." The name of it had given it away that I had no mother and no father, that I was parentless. I couldn't have her thinking I was an orphan; she already knew too much. Turning my eyes from right to left, I tried to decide which one of these little pine houses I was going to have her think was my home.

"Which house do you live at, Jasmine?"

"I'll let you know when we're there. We're not even close to my house yet."

"Don't be silly. We're almost at your house. I know it's one of these three houses staring at me. I just can't remember which one I saw you entering."

"Are you stalking me? How would you know where I live then, Daphne? I have never brought you to my house before."

"Let's just say my loving mother Judith followed you when you refused a ride from her."

"Are you kidding me?" I said as I grabbed my stomach to reduce the pain.

"Are you okay? Do you want to rest for a bit? We're almost there, Jasmine."

"I can't breathe. My stomach."

"Take a deep breath. Here, sit here, do it with me." We both took one deep breath, hoping to release the cumber that persistently attacks me. Sitting on the sidewalk, hearing my stomach coil intensely, I asked myself who this young lady was, sitting next to me. Who has Daphne turned into? I founded hard to believe this was the girl who mocked my appearance the first time she saw me. Now she was sitting on the sidewalk with me, helping me. This young lady wasn't scared of me. She wasn't scared that I sat next to her while my body rubbed against hers. Supporting me, making me feel well was her mission. She wasn't taking no for an answer.

"The beings told me you would act this way."

"What way?"

"Like this, denying their power."

"They're animals. What do they know, Daphne?" Second-guessing the ability of the animals living under Harmony, I refused to believe that they were nothing more than animals. I have seen what they were capable of. Daphne has seen what they've done to their surroundings, and here I stand denying what my mother has told me existed.

"We paint an unrealistic picture of them that can never be true. It's all in our head, Daphne."

"Nope, it's not. They really are what I think they are."

"What are they really? It seems like you know everything about these creatures. I would love for you to explain to me what they really are. Because to me they're just a variation of our imagination."

"They are more than that. They are jinxes of hope. They can help you get better."

"None of their works has succeeded. It leaves them weak, powerless. If you believe that they are who you think they are, Daphne, that should be your proof that nothing can help me."

"We are the only ones who can see them in the formation of animals, and of course other real animals can too. Idealistic humans see them as humans as well. Other people can feel their intentions. They see them as the devil, which they're not. They are here to help people like you and I."

Was what Daphne telling me true? My mother spoke often of those kinds of beings. She told me the jinxes were dark angels that were brought back from the underworld to finish the work of the undead; some come back to do good and some remain bad. My mother strongly advised me to stay away from the jinxes. They were nothing but bad news according to her. Their purpose was to collect souls. Me being a child, I saw her beliefs as nonsense. She was a woman who speaks of the voodoo lifestyle frequently. She spoke to me of voodoo as if I was an adult. I never took her stories of the paranormal seriously. If I ever come in contact with a jinx, she told me I would know; I should just follow my instincts.

The bad jinxes quicken the death of the ill, collect their soul, and bring them straight to the underworld. Once they find you, they never leave your side. They can appear in many forms, she said. Some appear in the form of a normal family; you see them with kids, husbands, doing normal daily things. They can also appear in cat form, chasing you in every direction until they can collect. If my memory serve me right, my mother was right, because I had been seeing a cat following me days prior to my death. Everything she spoke to me about the jinxes I had seen. Now I really didn't know if they were the jinxes, but her explanations seem to agree with the things Daphne explained and what I have experienced myself.

The first thing that notifies you of jinxes was the ability to understand the language of the animals. According to my mother, these animals were the squirrels, the swans, and the birds. She had said to watch out for these kinds of things, never to ignore something that appeared beyond to me, never to get too close to something unseen or unheard of. Her exact words were "Stay away, I tell you, stay away." She spoke of them as if she's been exposed to them. Maybe they were the reason behind why our family was cursed, thinking about it now. She also spoke of the good jinxes, which were protégé jinxes that prevent the bad ones from destroying the lives of others. They appeared in many forms of animals. It is very hard to distinguish between the bad and the good ones, she says. The creatures I have come in contact with have not done anything to hurt me but, rather, used their powers to help me.

"You ready to go now? I have to head back to school. My mom is picking me up soon."

"All right, let's go." Walking unevenly, it was time I told Daphne that what she called me the first day of school had some truth to it. I was homeless, begging the owner of the orphanage to allow me to stay until death strikes. Behind the girl that was suffering from the hand of a faceless man was Jasmine Pierce, the girl with AIDS, struggling to survive each day. There was nothing else to hide. She knew me now, and to me it was more than okay.

"You see this brick house that reads, 'Nelson's Orphanage'?"

"Yes, I see it," she replied.

"Well, that's my home. Guess you were right when you called me the homeless girl."

"There's nothing wrong with living at an orphanage."

"I'm an orphan! I live in a crowded house along with twelve people that barely wants to be around me."

"And I live in a crowded building with one hundred other people. I guess that makes me an orphan as well," she says to me, laughing with humor.

"Really, I can't imagine you being an orphan. The girl who takes constant trips to the land of dreams."

"There'll be none of those anymore. Pretty soon they'll kick us out too. My mother is running out of money," Daphne said while holding my waist to prevent me from falling. After telling her the truth of where I really lived and who I really was, I felt relieved that finally I was no longer hiding anything from her. The one person I've come to love, whom I found friendship in, had accepted me for who I really was. She knew of my disease, and my identity was known to her. She knows now who Jasmine Pierce really is. I wasn't a prostitute like they have said. I wasn't sleeping around with men I didn't know. To her I was a girl who was unlucky, running out time to keep the jinxes from collecting my forgotten soul.

Arriving at the orphanage, Daphne knocked on the door, shouting, "Open up!" I prayed Christina would be in her room, but there she came opening the door for none other than Daphne, the girl she made sure had a miserable life at school. Christina was everything that Daphne once were at. They both stood in front of each other with their jaws open. Christina shut the door, leaving her and I outside. Shortly upon closing the door, she opened the door again headstrong, asking Daphne, "What are you doing here?"

"I'm dropping her off. She's not feeling well."

"Yeah, we know! She's suffering from AIDS. She's dying soon."

"Well, I just thought I'd help her get home safe."

"You do know she has HIV, right?"

"Yeah, and what's your point?"

"Why do you attach yourself to her? She's contagious."

"To you she is. To me she's not. Can you help me get her inside, please?"

"I'm not touching her."

"I didn't know you live here."

"I don't! I volunteer here."

"Oh you do?"

"Yes, I do. I like to help the needy. It looks good on my resume for when I become an official American resident."

"How can you volunteer here when you're scared to be touched by Jasmine? Aren't you afraid of getting infected?" Daphne said while batting her eyes forcefully.

"I work with the other ones instead. She remains in her little room where nobody touches her."

Soon after Christina says she worked at the orphanage, Carole comes in, interrupting their conversation. She was in the kitchen, listening the whole time. She asked, "You work where, Christina?"

Daphne responded by saying, "She says she works here at the orphanage."

Christina ran to her room, slamming her door. And the truth shall set you free is what I tell you. She's been caught; running to her niche couldn't save her. Daphne was about to find the truth about her rich made-up life. If I was brave enough to speak a word, I would try to defend her. The churning of my empty stomach wouldn't allow it.

"No, you must have heard wrong. She lives here." Carole chuckled as she repeated that to Daphne.

"Wow, I didn't know this. She says the gold mansion was where she lives at."

"I have been taking care of Christina for ten years now. I think I know where she lives. This is her home."

"Why would she lie and say the mansion was hers?" There were many answers to that question. She was too good for an orphanage; having people believe she was a resident of America was easier. With a dried mouth, I forced myself to speak a word, wanting to get to bed to rest. "Help . . . m-me to my room."

"Oh yes, yes, let's get her in," Carole replied.

"She's really sick, ma'am," she said to Carole, forgetting I was using her thin frame as support.

"Call me Carole, honey."

"She's been throwing up blood, and her nose won't stop bleeding. I'll be surprised if she makes it another day, Carole."

"Put her here." Browsing my room, she asked Carole, "Can I volunteer here?"

"Oh nah, honey. We don't want to get you sick now. I want you to take those clothes you're wearing and wash them with hot water after you get home. Go on now. You're too pretty to get sick."

"I don't get sick easily."

"I'll keep that in mind. Thanks for helping Jasmine today. I appreciate it.

"Now why would this girl lie about where she lives? I know I raised her better than this. This orphanage is not that bad," Carole says to herself. She left my room shouting Christina's name, wanting to know why she was bad-mouthing the place that puts a roof above her head. Opening the door for us was her mistake. Once she settled down, she would make sure everyone suffered from my mistake, especially knowing how the *owner was her father.* She'd used that to her advantage.

"Why would you lie to this girl about living at an orphanage? I raised you kids better than this. Never forget where you come from."

"Because it's an orphanage. No one wants live here, Carole. Me personally, I don't want to live here anymore. It automatically identifies me as an orphan. I don't want to be an orphan."

"Don't you see all those kids sleeping on the streets at night? They would want nothing more than to have a comfortable bed to sleep in at night instead of a ceramic pavement that makes their bodies ache. That's very unappreciative of you. I thought I knew you, Christina."

The orphanage may have defined Christina, changed her to be something unpleasant to her surroundings, but it didn't define me. It made me stronger. Through it I valued what most kids on the streets wished for—a home of serenity; inside I could close my eyes and hope with everything I had. Rather, the faceless man that haunted me in the darkness of my room defined me; it defined me from what was real and what wasn't. When I was under Harmony's grace he had no power over me; there was no room to make me run away from myself. His greatest bet was when loneliness and susceptibility empowered me, Jasmine Pierce; that was when he sought the helpless girl he perpetually chased.

Time flew quickly, quicker than I could imagine. As the soul of the ill continued to mimic its origin, my lifeless body prepared itself for what's ahead. My eighteenth birthday was days away, days that I couldn't stop from moving in rapidly. For the first time since entering the orphanage, Mr. Nelson entered my room, not to wish me well but to serve me with my date of departure. He knocks on my door and says, "Your eighteenth birthday is coming soon. Do you know when you'll be able to move out?" What kind of question was that? He knew I had no one to go to. Death was what I was waiting for. I didn't have time to think about when or where I'm moving out. Mr. Nelson looked at me. "The only thing I'm waiting for is my soul to be taken away. I have nothing."

"After you turn eighteen I'm allowing you to stay for two weeks longer. After that you need to leave. I have already gotten someone else to move in," said Mr. Nelson.

You'd think after that breakdown from Christina he would rethink his demeanor, but no, Mr. Nelson was Mr. Nelson—remorseless and merciless. "I will pack my things once the time is up. Thank you for the extra two weeks you have given me to gather my things up."

"I only want the best for you, Jasmine. I hope you don't think I'm a bad person," he said as he turned his back, calling Christina. "Christina? Christina! Christina!" he shouted three times. "I'm coming!" Christina replied. Since he made his announcement, he hasn't shown his face around as much as he used to. A coward like him worked hard to avoid facing his problems. Christina has done nothing but become more of a diva; her attitude worsened. No one could reach her level. Level of what, I don't know. Maybe it was the level of needing an attitude readjustment. Carole cooks her food. It wasn't good enough. Her clothes needed to be ironed even when they were wrinkle free. At school she was going to America almost every weekend. She took the news of Mr. Nelson as her long-lost father to another level.

"What do you want? Do have another announcement you haven't told me yet?"

"Why do you choose to talk to me like this?" he said to her.

"I can talk whichever way I want," I overheard Christina saying.

"I have some good news for you."

"Really, are you taking me to America?" said Christina.

"No, no, not just anyone can go there, sweetie. I have something even better."

"What could be better than going to America?"

"Where are you getting this America story from? I have never heard you speak a word of America."

"My friend says all my problems would disappear if I go there."

"It's not that easy, Christina. If going to America is what makes you happy I would get you there in a heartbeat if I could."

"Of course, you can't. I wasn't expecting you to say you can anyway."

The land of grace sufficed to compensate for the time lost with a father according to Christina. She's trying hard to provide proof to her dearest Charlene is what she was doing. Daphne, who knows now of her dirty little secret, had threatened to expose her, and she couldn't have it. Daphne knew she was an orphan, and it was time to expose her for who she was in front of the school. What an irony. What goes around comes around is what's waiting to occur. Karma is a bitch, let me assure you of that.

"I don't want to be here anymore, Mr. Nelson."

"That's what I want to talk to you about actually, but all this talk of America is preventing me from saying it."

"You are going to get me out of here?"

"Yes, I am. Can you call me 'father' and not by my name?"

"I'm calling you 'Mr. Nelson.' Take it or leave it."

"Okay. Your eighteenth birthday is coming soon, and I was thinking you can come live with me."

"You want me to come live with you? I don't know what to say."

"Just says yes, my darling."

"Yes, I will come live with you. Now this is something to be blithe about," she said happily. She now found a new home. She wanted to move out of this place since I can remember. Christina once thought finding her mother would solve all of her problems. Getting her out of this place was why she was infatuated with finding her mother. She got her wish. She got out of the orphanage just like she wanted, not with the help of her mother, but with the help of someone else, her estrange father. She now has a father who had his own business. He made a lot money owning this orphanage. He was in charge of all the charity money that was offered to us; let's just say the money that is received is never the money we get. He is a smart man who knows greed. Christina certainly inherited that "gift" and many more habits from him. They didn't have real feelings; they only had feelings that accommodated themselves and one another. As one life survives, another falls apart.

It looked like the anger was gone between the new relatives; my madness was just only the beginning. When she goes to school, she was more in control than ever. With my eighteenth birthday ahead, I went to school even when Carole insisted not to. As the end of a new month approached, I was persistent to make the best of it even when the best means losing myself in the process. My mission was to spend as much time needed with my friends, meaning Daphne, and maybe the animals that I had many questions about.

"I see you made it in today. How are you feeling?" Daphne asked me.

"I'm all right."

"That's what I like most about you, always all right even when your face tells me differently."

"Are you planning on going to Harmony today?" I asked her.

"No, today I'm staying in school. I need to face reality. My life is different now. I can't keep running away from it. It's never going to be like it once was. You should too."

With a father in solitary prison, she couldn't have chosen any better words to say. She now had to work toward getting the fancy clothes she once wore to school, invoking jealousy from others. Her plan B was in progress. I was still searching for my plan B; it was not easy to find.

"I could use a break from Harmony." In grave condition, feet out and swollen, I nervously agreed to Daphne's proposal. Some sleep is what I could really use. Being at the paranormal grace of Harmony was the only place that guaranteed that. I was comfortable with Daphne, yet I felt the need to impress her.

"I think I will," I replied to her.

"We can have lunch at the cafeteria finally. I can't stand the odor of that bathroom," Daphne replied.

"If you had been in there for as long as I have I can guarantee you this odor would be avoidable."

"Check twelve o'clock. It's Christina," said Daphne.

"Why is she coming toward us?" I asked her.

"Probably to tell me off. I know the real her now, and the school doesn't. Picture you and I bribing her. We could get anything we wanted from her. Or we could just torture her just for the heck of it. We can ruin her just like she ruined you."

As comforting as it was to spend a day in the limelight, torturing my nemesis, I simply couldn't. With a few weeks left at her father's orphanage, she had more advantage than I did. School was the only atmosphere Daphne shared with Christina. I, on the other hand, shared a home with her, which her father owned. I wasn't afraid of Christina or maybe I was. Seeing her coming our way, the suspense couldn't get any more intense. She's not Christina, daughter of Samuel Nelson, for nothing. She often had something up her sleeve that would leave me furious.

"My dad needs you to start packing your things out tonight," Christina said.

"Packing my things? I spoke to him the other day, and he gave me another two weeks to find a place."

"You think you're the only one with tricks up their sleeve? You think wrong," Daphne indicated to Christina as she got closer to her face.

"Stay out of this. Let this be a warning to you," Christina replied.

"What's going on?" Charlene quickly barged into the conversation out of nowhere. I assume she saw the rich girl talking to her archrival and decided to get to the bottom of it. If the conversation continued, she will get to the bottom of her journey to America for sure. We all had a mission in this forsaken town. For some of us it was the journey to America, and for others it was finding a home to live in the next day, and for me, Jasmine Pierce, it was the miracle to fight the odds of the unnerving AIDS.

Christina pulled Daphne aside, leaving me with Charlene. She looked at me up and down with the intention of shoving me against the locker. The only reason why she didn't was because now I had a friend. That's how most of the students were; they pick on the lonesome and the ones that didn't fit their criteria of beauty. I fit all of the above. Chewing her gum loudly, she forced a couple of words to come out of the mouth. "You think you're something now, right? Just because Daphne speaks to you, huh?" Christina taught her well, or Daphne taught her well, or the thinking that Christina will bring her to America had her ego skyrocketing. She spoke like a replica of Christina. "I don't know. What do you think?" I asked her, feeling confident I could outshine her. She saw the weakness in me; upon entering this school I was never good at speaking for myself. There was always something occurring to show I was afraid to put out my true feelings. She continued to chew her gum loudly as she approached me. She flicked her thumb across my forehead and told me, "I could just snap you in two right now. Look at you. Is it freezing in here?"

"Well . . . I . . . ," I attempted to say to her.

"Huh, huh, who says you could say anything to me? Certainly not me," she said as she raised her hands, blocking my face. She was another one who thought it was a privilege to talk to her.

Christina and Daphne returned from their conversation, which couldn't be heard by Charlene or I. "Are you two best friends now?" Charlene asked. If I didn't know any better I'd say I sense some jealousy coming from Charlene. It wasn't a jealousy of losing her best friend; it was more of "I'm losing my place in line for America" jealousy. "Me and her? You must be out of your mind," Christina replied.

"Okay, good! Because I can't afford to lose my best friend."

"She's not going anywhere. Let's leave these two losers alone."

"So you never told me how your trip to America went," I heard her asking Christina from a distance. "Oh, that. It was fun. We have math together this period," Christina replied.

159

"I can't wait till we can go together," Charlene said. I wonder how this conversation ended. Christina didn't want to talk about America because she has been nowhere near that country.

"What did you two speak about?" I requested of Daphne.

"I have bad news. She says if I tell anyone about seeing her at the orphanage, she will tell the whole school you contracted AIDS through prostitution."

"What did you tell her?"

"Don't worry. She's bluffing."

"I don't think I want to say in school today. I don't feel well."

"Do you want me to bring your homework?"

"No, it's okay. I'll take them when I come back tomorrow."

"Feel well soon," she said to me when we both knew no such thing will happen. See, with Christina, the word "bluffing" doesn't exist. Her words were a ploy to dictate how in control she was of everyone. She means what she says. Daphne doesn't back down, nor does she let people control her. It was in my own hands now. Taking control of the situation was what I had to do. That being said I didn't want to be around to hear Christina make her huge announcement. I didn't want to be around to witness the humiliation in front of hundreds of students, seizing the day they saw my weakness.

April 2 was my eighteenth birthday. After years of struggling and being parentless, my day for departure was here. My days to join the kids sleeping on the cold pavement were here, and my seven-month deadline was just days nearing. Eighteen was a big number for me, very important, especially for Mr. Nelson and the law. I was now out of their hands. I was no longer their responsibility anymore. With contentment comes anguish coming from my side.

"Today is a special day," said Carole, who had baked a cake with butter to replace cream. "I wouldn't say a special day," I replied to her.

"I baked you a cake."

"What's the point of baking me a cake when I will regurgitate shortly after? I can't keep anything in my stomach anymore."

"You're leaving soon. Maybe you can cut cake with your friends here at the orphanage." My friends? Why does that seem fake to me? Ryan, who seldom talked to me, now remained mute. Rodney, who once helped me to my bed hadn't since said a word to me, and Christina, who I went to the same school with, was contemplating of ways to humiliate me in front of the whole student body. What friends? There were twelve kids in the house; none has acknowledged my presence, so what friends were she speaking of? Daphne didn't leave the house. I could have assumed she meant her by the term "friends." Friends were something I was just beginning to adjust to before my life was suddenly cut short.

"Kids, come chant 'Happy Birthday' to Jasmine."

They all came running from outside happy; unfortunately this blissful moment wasn't for the fact that I turned eighteen. It was for the butter cake. "Can I eat my cake first before Jasmine, Carole?" Ryan asked.

"It's her birthday. She should get the first bite, don't you think?"

"If she gets the first bite, I won't eat it."

"Why not?"

"Because I don't want to eat her leftovers."

"It's okay. Go ahead, you kids. I can't eat it anyway. Celebrate for me, will you, Ryan?" I replied.

"She said she doesn't want the cake," Ryan said to Carole.

"Are you sure?" said Carole.

"I'm sure. I'm going to bed. I don't feel well."

"You never feel well," Rodney said. He couldn't have chosen any better words. I never felt well. "That's because she has AIDS," replied Ryan.

"Okay, enough with this conversation. Just eat the cake."

"Everyone already knows she has HIV," Christina added as she stood by the table, licking the cake off her hands.

"Who have you told about this, Christina?" Carole asked. If she could tell the whole word of my disease she would. Opportunity hasn't struck yet. She never backed down against her words, and from what Daphne has told me, watching my back was the only thing I could do. She will lose no chance at taking me down. She couldn't stand the idea of seeing me happy. Constant torture was worth a lifetime to Christina.

"No one, but sooner or later they will know the truth for good. She can't just keep walking around infecting everyone. It is very selfish on my part, knowing the outcome of keeping silent."

No longer waiting for the magic number eighteen, what was left to do now was to plan my next move. I was very indecisive. I knew what my next step was. It was easy as one, two, three. I just didn't know if I should get ready for my hole or to start packing for the streets of darkness once again. The streets were what got me in my condition, and now I was looking back to it again. My mother had no known family member that I could stay with. Auntie Annabel was the only family member that I knew of, but she was so far gone. Her path was too dark to follow. While people call me a prostitute, dying from HIV, my auntie Annabel was in that direction. If they say prostitution is what causes HIV then was my auntie Annabel going through it? Was she passing the disease to the men she lays with in the back of those wooden trucks? My auntie isn't herself, and I wasn't myself for those reasons. Two struggles and two similar stories all passing through the eyes of darkness. As one journey approaches its end, another one begins.

Commencing to gather the little things I had to leave the orphanage with, Carole knocked on my door with one hand hiding behind her back. "I have a surprise for you," she said. Nothing could be a surprise to me at that moment. The only thing that would be a surprise was finding a way to wake up from this never-ending nightmare. Now that would be some surprise, but until then nothing suffices.

"I have managed to get you a bottle of those pills you needed," Carole said. A while ago I would have jumped for it, but now it didn't faze me any longer. Those pills were the reason why my relationship with Carole had been so distant, and I vowed to be free of drugs until death do me part. I was going to die with or without the pills anyway. My fate had been made up by the judge, the doctor and almost by everyone around me.

"You didn't need to waste your money on those. You can throw it on the bed if you wish," I said to her while tying the plastic bag that held my clothes.

"What's going on? You don't seem too happy about your gift. It's the medication that brings you comfort." Seeing it now, these pills weren't pills of comfort. They were a trap assembling me for disaster. Those pills came with consequences. For instance, pushing me away from who I was. I saw things differently, looking at my trembling image. With those pills, the mirror showed me who the HIV and the pills together were turning me into—a walking zombie on the verge of following my mother's road to destruction. This wasn't her dream. She wanted me to be something better than her, teach those who have overcome so much to strive to the top successfully. And that was her motto for her only daughter. Her death was unexpected and so was my sudden HIV news. We were a family full of surprises, and now I'm okay with it. A while back it was a curse, but now I see it differently, a blessing.

"I see you're already packing," Carole said.

"What's left to do? Mr. Nelson has already given me a deadline and so has Christina, the co-owner of this orphanage."

"She's moving out soon too. Mr. Nelson is taking her."

"I'm aware of that. How can I forget?"

"You still have twelve days left in here. You don't need to start packing."

"I'm packing because Mr. Nelson could change his mind anytime now before this final day comes."

"Well, these clothes need to be washed anyway. I'm not going to let you leave with dirty clothes."

"But I already packed them," I told Carole. Her doing favors for me was the last thing I needed. The feeling of being an obligation to her kicks in again.

"It's okay. We can pack them again. I'll pack them up myself." I took the clothes out of the bag nervously.

"I can't believe I'm leaving this place soon. It feels like I've been here forever."

"Come with me. I have a new treatment I want to try on you. This one is odorless," Carole said.

It was odorless, but my body refused its meaning. Nothing helped anymore. Nothing was worthy enough for these two demons that seize my life. Just like the spreading of the AIDS, the man got stronger. With my senses shut, I've learned to avoid the demographics of them all. If I ever hated myself, regretting the very birth of myself that day was one of those days that made me realize eighteen was the last age I would ever see. Convincing is what I needed to assure myself that this would be over soon. My mother was waiting for me, and I was waiting to see her again after ten years. I didn't know which side she was waiting for me, but she was waiting for me.

A night spent without sleep where a man finds the pleasure of following my every turn and twist was never my ideal way of staying awake at night, a night filled with nightmares and flashbacks of what's already been done to me; destroying the dreams and hopes of my future was never an ideal way of waking up in the morning either. It doesn't matter how I put it. It sounds ugly either way. With baggy and bloodshot eyes and dark circles ravishing themselves through the outer layers of my eyes, I look like I just turned fifty years old. I was often mistaken for a much older person when I was fifteen. Now that I'm eighteen one can only imagine what my face captivated before I took my last breath. It captivated the need for rest, the need for the reincarnation of a mother, it captivated loss and helplessness. So many things seen through the eyes of an eighteen-year-old girl before she actually reaches womanhood. My innocence was taken from me when I was thirteen, and for that I have been convicted as a prostitute.

My mother was ripped from my bare hands when I was just nine, and from there my world shattered. Everything suddenly became meaningless, unworthy.

For years my memories served me as a mockery of things I will never get a chance to have, and then for years my shadows took over my head, taunted by a devious faceless man who left me traumatized, paralyzed throughout my youth. After my mom's life was cut short, he plunged in to fill the void with darkness. His comfort was nowhere else but inside my head. A pill couldn't get rid of it. Carole's homemade medicines couldn't get rid of, but for the short time I was with Harmony, he disappeared, intimidated by the power of other beings. The jinxes were the reason for my stability. They sacrificed their own well-being for mine. I call them jinxes because I know now my mother was right.

"Do you want to go to school today?" Carole asked. Harmony has been calling me for days now, and that's where I'll be getting my education today. Some rest is what was strongly needed by my weakening posture. Going to school was not going to get me what I needed. I told her I was planning on going when I really was going somewhere else. "Yeah, I'll be going," is what I told her. The entire night I was thinking of Harmony. I could no longer hold my eyes anymore. Sleeping was the food I asked for. It was something I didn't need to worry about turning to blood or regurgitating it.

"Don't believe her. All she does is skip school. I rarely see her in school anymore," Christina told Carole as she brushed her brown locks. *Maybe I wouldn't have to skip school if you didn't spend hours of making a fool out of me*, I said to myself. She was one of the major factors why I avoided school. She had an army poking the little life out of me. "Is this true?" Carole asked. It was true. Scared of her reaction, I lied. "She's lying."

"What reason do I need to lie about you?" Christina replied.

"For someone who doesn't care, you sure have a lot of concern," I told her.

"My only concern is that you don't infect my father's house with your AIDS. That's the only concern you'll ever get from me.

"Bye, Carole. My dirty clothes are on my bed. My father wants you to wash them." Since when did Carole wash Christina's clothes? With a newfound father comes power to her. She can now boss the woman who keeps this orphanage together.

"Your father never told me anything about washing your clothes, Christina. I just spoke to him on the phone last night."

"I just spoke to him now. He told me to tell you that. Don't be mad at me. I'm only the messenger. I also told him I saw you washing AIDS girl's clothes. He doesn't want you to hang them the same place you hang my clothes."

"All right."

"He's afraid of losing her only daughter to AIDS, that's why. Any concerns, take it up with my father."

She spoke to Carole as if she was one of her little puppets from school. Carole was too old to be spoken down to. The diva attitude has gotten far over her head after discovering she was to escape the orphan lifestyle. She had a father pampering her, but that shouldn't be any reason to treat the woman who has been taking care of you for a decade. Everything she wanted, she got, except one thing, reaching the land of America. I wondered how Little Miss Diva would feel if she got to the free land. I can picture her being more of a narcissistic girl, controlling almost everyone crossing her path.

With Christina watching her every move, she had no choice, but to allow herself to be talked down to by a child. Her world now revolves around her if she needed to keep her job. Christina was her surveillance; she was a slave to her commands. Carole fears losing her job. It was be talked down to her or work 18 hours at the farm everyday making little money. She didn't like working there at all. It was only a place to make a little extra when the kids aren't around, that's how it was, but when I arrived at the house she finds herself working there very often to help support my medical bills.

"I'm off to school now. My father is coming over tonight to help me gather my things," replied Christina.

"Please tell me again what she just said about skipping wasn't true."

"It's not true."

"I'm going to find out. I'm taking you to school."

"I don't feel well enough for school."

"Yes, you're going to school. When you're on the street, you can choose not to, but for now you're going. You just told me you were fine to go."

"I need rest, Carole."

"You kids think you can walk all over me. Well, not anymore. This stops now."

"Get in the car." After learning Christina was Mr. Nelson's kid, Carole demanded that he fix her wagon. Her excuse was Christina was afraid of walking to school. If it was Jasmine who was afraid of walking to school, it would have been a different story. If the house needed anything, Christina was the weapon she used. It would have been wrong to have his daughter walking to school, fearing danger, as if this was problem before. The reason she's such a diva is because our lives depended on her.

I got into the car scared. This brought me back to when I was in third grade, when my mother went to my school, embarrassing me in front of my peers, asking who dared taunt me. I was really young back then. The kids didn't really know much about the feeling of embarrassment; they make fun of me now because of that incident; the next day it's forgotten about, off with the next ploy it was to them. Being eighteen in a school surrounded by young adults who starves for America, it was different. The entire school knows me. I was just a hot pot in the back of their head; glimpses of my face awaken their comical tendencies. I was quickly identified as a joke to them.

Courage was never a strength of mine. In the car I could have put an end to Carole's madness. The strength to do so was blocked within me. I couldn't find it in me to hit break. Unevenly was how she was driving on the road. From one side to another side she was driving like a madwoman pressing me to prove Christina wrong.

"It's really not my plan to go to your school, pulling your professor out in the midst of her teaching to find if you're lying to me or not. Christina has no reason to make up something like this."

"Carole, I did that once. She doesn't like me. At school her act is 'I don't know her.' She's a very mean person."

"What reason do you have to skip school? When I was your age the penalty for something like that was beating." And she went on and on about how I should let nobody persecute me to this level. Her and my mother had something in common too—they didn't go to school because they couldn't afford education. Instead they stayed with their parents, aiding with the farmwork, she says. Free education was never something that existed during their time; only the rich and the privileged were fortunate for such a gift, she explains. To them education is now a necessity, not an onus. Stuck with their old-fashioned ways, they became strictest to the ones who neglect literacy. She was angry at me, angry at the idea of lies, taking for granted what she didn't have the opportunity to do decades into the past.

If I tried to explain to her why I ignored school she would never understand. Experiencing what I went through may be the only way she would understand; a woman who starves for a high diploma can never logically understand the reasons behind my actions. Skipping school was a requirement, a must; the bathroom had no room for responsibilities like mine anymore.

"We're about to find out if Christina is lying about you."

Shyly I got out of the beat-up wagon with everyone staring at me. I loved Carole; her will to see me overcome this disease was effortless. However, when she entered the school, nothing was ever the same again. It wasn't her; it was everyone else.

She entered math class and requested to speak with the professor in private. "Can I speak to you in private?" she said.

"I see you brought Jasmine to class. It's about time she comes to class," the professor said.

"Is there any chance we can go outside to speak about this situation?"

"I have to start class, ma'am."

"This will only take a few minutes."

"All right." I fixed myself to grab my seat when she grabbed my and hand said, "You're coming with me too."

"One of my kids says that she hasn't been showing up to school. I'm here to confirm this matter."

"May I ask who?"

"Christina Precilien."

"She's one of my students too, a darling. Her I can only remember once when she didn't show up to class. She's always present. Great kid too. It is my pleasure to work with her," the professor said to Carole.

With my head bowed, only great things were said of Christina. As long as they kept talking about her, I was fine. It gave me time to think about how I was going to explain myself to Carole later. "She is just adorable," said the professor. If she lived with her I'm sure she wouldn't think she was adorable or if she was ailing like I she would see her differently. "On the other hand, Ms. Carole, I'm afraid I can't say the same for Jasmine. She will not graduate if she keeps up with what she's doing right now."

"She told me Christina was lying when she told me that she hasn't been attending school."

"Let me be the one to tell you Christina was telling you the truth."

"So is that how it is now, Jasmine? Who are you? It's like I don't even know you anymore." With my head bowed, my jacket covering my exterior head, I responded to her, "Sorry, I won't do this again."

"Another thing, her hygiene needs to be maintained. She wears the same thing four days a week. Quite frequently the kids pick on her very often about that."

"That will be taken care of from now on. My main concern right now is her grades," Carole replied.

"I'm sorry, Jasmine. I don't mean to hurt your feelings, but something has to be done about this. I'm very happy she took the time to be here today. It was about time someone does so."

"Don't feel sorry for me. I'm only passing by," I told her sadly.

"It's too late to do anything about her grades, Ms. Carole. What we can do is have her come to school from now on for class participation. I guarantee she'll spend next semester here again." Huh! Next semester. Let's see. Next semester I'll be in a hole identified by digits on my tombstone. Next semester, if what Carole has taught me about the afterlife is true, I'll either be sitting at the right of God with my mother or I'll be sharing the same place with Satan. I don't know; it can go either way, I thought to myself. I'm going to die without a diploma, just like my mother. That's not what I wanted for myself, but that's the reality, and I did die without it. The faceless man turned and refused to see the best side of me. As they were talking among themselves about my hygiene and my lack of interest in education, I spoke to myself. I walked a mile away to shower every day. My professor thought maybe I wasn't taking showers before coming to school. Wrong. I did, but the zits, the pimples, the blisters hidden underneath my oversized jacket told a deceitful story of my hygiene. I showed lack of interest in my schoolwork because picking a pencil forces the devil in my head of what I can't do. Showing this like in my education wasn't something I chose. I wasn't trying to be a rebel trying to prove to some people that I didn't need school; it was a path that was chosen for me by the faceless man.

He worked hard to keep me away from doing the things that my mother wanted for me.

"Is she ill? I have also heard some rumors around."

"What have you heard?"

"Rumors are going around she has cancer, but I know if she has cancer, you of all people would speak to the school administration about it."

"Oh she's fine. Like I said her hygiene will be taken care of. For the time being, I will make sure she gets to class. I will be taking her to class."

Charlene, who was late to class as always, saw the professor talking to Carole and smiled at me, not a valiant smile but a sinister smile.

Underneath that oversized jacket I was aware of everything around me. People may have thought I was a mute. I wasn't. I was keeping note of those who outraged me. So she left telling me, "And take this hood of your head. It's eighty degrees outside."

"Don't touch it," I told her. No one was allowed to touch my hood. Touching it brought out the indecency out of me. Not even Carole could touch it. My jacket kept me safe from the public, and no one could valiantly make me remove it. I remove it if I choose to. When the kids try to take it off my head, it always gets me angry. It was okay for them to poke me with their pens or throw paper balls at me, but when it comes to my jacket I became destructive inside that little head of mine. It was my most prized possession. It was mine; nobody could take it away from me. Just like the jinxes, it kept me safe. It took their place when I wasn't with Harmony. No one sees how my outer shell looks like but me.

I went into class after Carole left. Upon my entering the class, everyone's eyes were on me, giving me an obscene look. I sat down. I said nothing to block the whispers. I put my head down on the bench and shut my eyes, imagining being under Harmony. Their persnickety attitude could no longer be tolerated. With my oversized jacket I was able to block them. Charlene was there. She made sure the kids kept talking about me. She kept the conversation going. At one point her voice was the only one I could hear.

"I can smell her all the way from here," Charlene said, laughing with joy that I couldn't say anything back to her.

"Enough, Charlene!" the professor asked. Daphne wasn't in class that day. Weak and unable to defend myself, I thought about her also. Her reputation may have been tarnished, but she stands her ground. After the whole school learned of her downfall it made her more valiant. Not in the same circle of friends she once were, she pitied them as they pitied her. Charlene was a sordid individual seeking attention anywhere she could find it. It didn't bother her, even if it meant starting a fight with the most hazed girl at school. I was always her target because I was easy; I was weak and selfless.

At noon the bell rang, which meant it was time for lunch. That day ten dollars kept me from using the bathroom to spend my forty-five minutes of recess. For my eighteenth birthday, Carole gave me ten dollars, which I had forgotten about. On my way to the bathroom, I reached inside my pocket and felt a piece of paper on my black-gray jeans. I took it out to see what it was. It was the ten dollars that she had given me. The cafeteria food always smelled good. They served good food, but they were expensive, I tell you. The cafeteria was something the school was known for, their fresh produce and their skilled chefs. I turned around and went to the cafeteria, where I bought my lunch. With my ten dollars, since I was having difficulties swallowing, I bought one pudding, a bottle of pineapple juice, and two big spoons of rice, which all came to the amount of what I had in my pocket. Although I knew I wouldn't be able to digest the rice, I bought it anyway in an attempt to get some salt in my system. I thought maybe today was going to be my lucky day. I had ten dollars in my pocket, and I was about to eat a good meal, a meal other than rice and beans. Today was a day for something different. It has been a while since I could remember having something from the cafeteria.

Feeling somewhat confident, I browsed around for an empty bench. Good, I found one, I thought. Right toward the end, the perfect spot. It was a whole bench all to myself. Today was the day I would finally sit down at the cafeteria of the school I was attending. Some people tried their best to keep me from eating lunch at that cafeteria. However, not today. It was my lucky day, I'm thinking, envisioning a perfect lunch day. I walked there, put my lunch down, took my bags, which weighted tons of pounds, and settled it on the other side of the bench to have people think it was occupied. Finally I thought I was going to sit down and enjoy a satisfying meal. So I'm eating my pudding when out of nowhere I see Charlene, Christina, and her soccer friends coming toward my direction. "Please don't come this way, please don't come my, please, please," I repeated to myself. Doesn't matter how many pleases I was repeating; they were still coming in my direction with their plates of food on their hands. My heart raced out of my chest. Something was up, I could feel it. My breathing became heavy; I couldn't slow it down. Showing signs of fear, Charlene said, "Look at her. We haven't even said anything to her yet she's already scared. Boo!"

"Why are you sitting here? Don't you know this is our reserved bench?"

"I don't know where you have been eating your lunch. Wherever it is though, I would go back there," Christina said, acting like she has never seen me before in her life.

"Yo! I'm hungry. You need to leave," her soccer friend said. Just like Daphne had taught me, when in deep stress, simply do a deep exhalation, in and out, and it would make everything go away. It would strengthen me up. I wasn't giving up that easy. I was sick of these people ordering me around. Without Daphne's presence it was time I challenged myself, put to use what she has taught me. I was going to defend myself alone no matter what the risks were. This was going around for way too long. If I was going to die soon, I might as well take this one last fracas. That was the strength in me, knowing I could die any day now. It was the right thing to do. Fight with the life in me, tell them something to remember me by.

"I'm not leaving. I was here first."

"What did you say?" Charlene responded.

"I'm not leaving, I said. Are you deaf!"

"You know what? Keep it. I'm out of this drama. Guys, let's bounce," said Sansoux to his other teammates.

"No, guys, don't leave!"

"Christina, you better handle this," Charlene said.

173

"Watch. She's going to leave."

"When she leaves, call us. We'll be sitting over there," Sansoux replied.

"Look, I'm not looking for any trouble. You have to leave."

"I'm not leaving, I said. I'm going to sit here and eat my lunch that I have spent ten dollars on, get it?" I took a spoon of my rice followed by a sip of my pineapple drink. Again I already knew the need to throw up was going to happen. I felt uncomfortable trying to hold it in.

"Look at her face. She's turning purple. She looks like she going to throw up. Move back, you guys, I think she's going to puke," said Charlene.

"No, she's not. I live with her, and she does that ugly face of hers very often when she eats. Don't pay attention to it," Christina says.

"Wait, what? You never told me you lived with her. She lives in that gold mansion with you? What a privilege."

"Wait, no, no! That's not what I meant." And just like that the truth came out. I didn't say it, Daphne didn't say, it was her who said it. Those words came out of her mouth. They didn't intentionally come out, but they came out. The truth was bound to come out somehow.

Coughing nervously, I said, "It's true. She lives with me, and she doesn't live in that gold mansion. She lives at Nelson's Orphanage with me. She's never been to America, and she never will."

Disturbed, Charlene told her, "Please tell me she's lying. Tell me you're not an orphan."

Cat got her tongue. Disturbed also for exposing her own secret, she was unable to speak. She looked as if she's just seen a ghost. Charlene shook her and said, "Please tell me she's lying right now!"

Out of her frozen zone, she said, "What do you think, Charlene?"

"I don't want to think I've been friends with an orphan, that's for sure!"

"Unfortunately, I am an orphan, and I've been sharing an orphanage with her."

"What did I tell you? People with mansions like that don't come to school here," Julmina said to Charlene.

"I should have believed you. She always made up some excuse when I asked if I could come in."

"She's a liar."

"Why lie to me? How could you do something so thoughtless, Christina!"

"You want to know more, Charlene? I have no mother, and I just found out that I have a deadbeat father that knew of my existence but never stopped to think of me."

"You're garbage! I always thought you were a poor excuse to society. Yes, you might be pretty, but you're not all that. I can see that now."

"Thank you, I may gladly add. You want to know more? All this talk about America, taking you with me, it was all a lie. Even if I could, I would never take you."

"You will never get away with this!"

"I don't care what you do to me. I'm leaving this godforsaken town, and I'm never coming back"

"Is that another lie too? You'd be doing all of us a favor."

"I don't care if you believe or don't believe me. I'm glad all of this came out. I was getting tired of trying to impress you people anyway."

"You people? I'm the best thing that ever came into your life."

"You're like a disease, Charlene. You spread and spread till you destroy."

Stuck in the middle of a feud again, I wanted to find the next latrine or the next trash barrel to vomit in. Their feud had no meaning to me. While all this was going on, Harmony was the voice that adhered to my head. I got up and grabbed my bag. As I made a move to walk away from the scene, Christina says, "Hey, where are you going? You caused all this. Now it's my turn. I will tell them what you've been hiding from the school." She grabbed me by the branch of my bag and said, "Sit here, this is not over!" Shaken by what she's about to do, I accidentally regurgitate an inch away from Charlene's foot. "You better get away from me before I do something I might regret! I swear to God," she said with piercing eyes, ready to do the unthinkable. With her hands clenched tightly, I told her, "I'm sorry, I didn't mean to do it," fearing what she might do to me.

Meanwhile, the whole cafeteria remained dummied up. Christina stepped on top of the bench and said, "Hey everyone, can I get your attention please? Over here, all eyes over here please." There were professors, students, and janitors all standing around to hear her announcement. Anywhere I turned my eyes for an easy escape, someone was already standing there with their hands wrapped around their chest. My jacket was on the other side of the bench. Even that was far away from me. There was nowhere to run or hide. My jacket couldn't save me.

"Now that I got your attention I have an announcement to make. Some of you may have overheard Charlene and I talking. Yes, I'm an orphan, but it appears I'm not the only one holding a secret. I have made mistakes but nothing compared to what I'm about to tell you."

"Christina, please don't do this," I pleaded to her.

"I'm apologizing beforehand. I have to do this."

"You don't have to! I'm truly remorseful for what I did!"

She pointed her fingers at me. "Ever since you got to the orphanage, you have ruined everything. Everything Carole used to do for me she no longer does them because she's too busy taking care of your disease-infested ass."

"That's not true. She does the same thing for you and I, for all of us."

"That's not what we see, especially Ryan. She doesn't take him to the park anymore because she's too busy working at the farm to provide for you! You took that away from him, you crazy lunatic."

"Christina, do what you like! Whatever you decide to tell these people, it's not going to change anything. Your life will stay the same, and so will everyone else's in here. You will still remain an ex-orphan."

"Oh I beg to differ. We'll just have to see, wont we?"

Stunned by her words, I sat down, ready for humiliation to strike once again. I could never redeem myself from this. I will forever remain in history as the eighteen-year-old woman who dealt with HIV, the young lady who spent time convincing people she wasn't a prostitute.

"Get down from there," a professor shouted from across the cafeteria.

"I will, but first I must reveal the Jasmine I know. I must put all the rumors to rest. You all had your assumptions that she was dealing with cancer. Today I will put all of these unanswered questions to rest. You see, Jasmine Pierce, this girl sitting right here, has AIDS. She's been walking around the school infecting everyone."

"What! She's only eighteen. How do we know you're not lying? You said you were a resident of America when all this time you were an orphan," Charlene added.

Stunned by Christina's accusations, Professor Eugene from art class screamed, "This is impossible!"

"You want proof? I'll show you!" What proof was she talking about? She got down from the bench and asked me, "Stand up!"

"No! I won't! What are you doing, Christina?"

"I need to give these people proof that I'm not lying!"

She held me up and ripped the buttons off my jacket. I refused to wear a shirt underneath that jacket because of the calescent atmosphere. I frequently wear simply the jacket. With my naked body exposed, everyone's jaw seemed to have dropped, staring at my thinning frame covered by warts and all kinds of pimples. There was no room for space in my body as the buttons settled on top of one another.

"Now do you believe me? She was a prostitute!"

Overwhelmed by what's been seen and heard, the whole cafeteria started talking all at once. Charlene, who was standing next to me at the time, ran away after what she had seen. Students who were getting ready to eat their meal quickly threw their food away.

"Now I'm done," Christina said as she walked away from me. Some students left the cafeteria, some stayed, staring at what I was going to do. Sickened and hurt by what Christina had done, I ran out of the cafeteria, thinking of never coming back. And from there I left school; not at any time did I ever look back. I vowed to never go back even if it meant running away again to another town to start my abridged life over again.

There was one place I was slightly safe to go, Harmony. It was calling me, I could hear it. On my way to Harmony the blisters that had formed on my body started popping one by one. Holding my jacket from displaying my front, I couldn't keep the pus from drenching my jacket. Touching the open blisters left me in constant pain. As one blister dries out, blood replaces it. Looking at my lifeless body I cried with dry eyes. A distance from Harmony, I felt like its road extended the closer I was to getting to it. My eyes saw an elongated road that never came to an end. My body has given up, the little electricity it had was fizzling out. I had to make it; there was no way I was going to lay on this road bare. Harmony was the place I needed to be at. I forced myself to jog even when the burning of my open blisters worsened.

My malady worsened when blood started running like the little canal that runs vigorously across Harmony. The thinning jacket had no space left to hold the fluids that's being sucked out of my shell. Usually I'd carry a cloth in my bag to help me block the coming of it. I left my bag at the school cafeteria; my jacket undercompensated for that. Each time I was near Harmony something happens to prevent me from getting there. My eyes blurred as I saw the jinxes coming.

Finally, after feeling like I have been working for hours to reach Harmony, I reached my destination. In the pond where I speak to my mother, Daphne was pondering in a delighted humble posture, staring into space. I grunted, coercing myself to cry out for her. Shocked by the severity of my current condition, she rushed out of the pond with only a T-shirt covering her upper body.

"What happened to you?" she asked me.

"I'm n-n-not going back," I said as I fell to the ground. And just like that, my soul removed itself from the ailing shell. My lifeless body that was driven to overcome the odds was gone.

"Jasmine, can you hear me?" she asked. I could hear her. I was talking too, but she couldn't see me nor hear me. "Daphne, Daphne, I'm okay, I feel great, and I'm cured," I said to her. She kept calling me even when I was speaking to her. That's when I realized it was my soul talking to her. And that's where the beginning of the story comes to play.

The jinxes assembled themselves, chanting, humanizing, trying to resurrect my lifeless body. With Daphne in the middle of their circle, I heard them saying, "Drag her here to the pond, drop her in the water." She struggled to carry me into the pond. With my lifeless body in her hand, I fell. There I was left feet away from the pond full of enlightens. Near there was a powerful present felt to core of my soul. With the jinxes still chanting, the vines from the bridge elongated; the oasis underneath covered my head while the vines of Harmony strapped my blistered body. In the soul I felt the power of coming into my flesh, but something was pulling me back, keeping my soul away from coming in contact with my exposed body.

"Jasmine, please wake up," I heard her say. While she pleaded for my resurrection, the beings convened to cure me, take me back from the afterlife. Getting closer to my body, my soul refused to enter its shell. Everything the jinxes tried didn't work.

The vines left my body, and to the jinxes that was the final call. There was no coming back from this. Daphne refused to accept the fact that I was never coming back again.

"When the vines leave, that's the sign that her heart stops."

"Keep chanting, she can't be dead!"

"I'm sorry, there's nothing I can do," one of the swans said.

"Is there something I can do?"

"Go to the orphanage, tell Carole of this news that Jasmine is no longer with her."

"Now I need you to do something for us. Close your eyes," a member of Lucid said.

"Will this help Jasmine?"

"Yes, it will. For your sake, it will."

She closed her eyes, hoping for what might be a miracle to bring her friend back. That's not what she received. Instead I got twelve individuals telling me my fight is now over on the other side. The beings I saw as squirrels, swans, and rabbits from the beginning were once humans too. They were humans who appeared as animals on the other side of life. They were jinxes but the good kind sent to me for protection. In the flesh, tragedy struck them also. I was their unfinished business, that's why the light skipped them years and years ago. Their mission is now complete.

"My name is Maxime."

Maxime was part of the swan group. She was always up front when it comes to providing comfort. She was the one who told Daphne she couldn't get any pulse from me. She was the one who gave the okay to start the ritual. Without her okay, nothing could be done. She's a ninety-year-old woman who held the power within. She was the key to every ritual that was done.

"May I ask how you died?"

"I died of the same thing you died from. We all died from HIV. It was the deadly disease that haunted us for years. Knowing what we went through, we didn't want you to go through this alone."

"You knew of me before then?"

"We saw how much love you had for animals."

"I do have a soft spot for them."

"We must show you how this bridge really looks like. Everything you and Daphne were seeing was a fantasy, and we wanted you to see it that way."

With a clear vision of the bridge, it was nothing compared to the soothing bridge I adored in my flesh. The pond was nonexistent. Where the pond once was located were hays for the horses that I now see. The long river that stretched seamlessly across the bridge is nothing but mud mixed with the defecations of the horses. As for Harmony itself there was nothing unique about it. It was a ruined bridge that's been out of order for decades. I wasn't even born yet. It was a forgotten bridge that ignited my pulse while looking for something to help me forget about the pain that came upon me continuously.

"Now that we have shown you the real image of Harmony, as you call it, we must go home now," Lisa says. Lisa was a member of the swans, a beautiful young girl who died from the hands of her father. She had an angelic presence that made my heart rejoice.

"One more thing," I asked them. "Was seeing my mother in the river real?"

"No, that was you who made that up. You missed her so much that you created a fantasy world of you and her. We don't have that power. It was your superstition."

"We thought you were crazy too, observing you speaking to the water," Maxime replied.

"We must go now. Our light is waiting for us," Lisa said.

Just like that their lights she'd upon their soul. Up and away they went. Daphne weeping over my body was not what I wanted. She ran to the orphanage and told Carole of the news that I was no longer living.

"Carole, Carole, open up!" She knocks.

"What's wrong? Why are you crying?" Carole asked her.

"It's Jasmine, she's dead." Carole drops to the floor, bursting in never-ending tears.

We all knew this day was coming. I didn't think that day would be today. There were many things I hadn't done. I planned on leaving my room spotless, I planned on making amends with everyone in the house, I planned to get the little brotherly connection that I once found with Ryan before I left. But then the unthinkable happened—death struck—disallowing me to do the things that I planned on doing in the next few days. Doesn't matter how much weeping was done in honor of Jasmine Pierce. My body still remained underneath the bridge, waiting for its identification numbers.

"Where is she now?" Carole asked.

"She's under the bridge. I can show you."

"What bridge are you talking about? The only bridge I know of is the Joule Bridge. Nobody should be going there."

"Jasmine and I have been going there for relaxation for months, if not a few years now, her longer than I. She knew of it before I did."

"I should have kept her home from school. I should have. This is my entire fault," Carole says.

"It's not your fault. It's no one's fault. I can tell you this, Carole. She is the strongest individual I've ever known. She fought till she couldn't anymore."

"She was strong. We must accept the fact she's watching over us now."

"That's the only thing we can do right now."

In a hole my body goes. Carole spent fifty-six dollars for that hole with the number identification. The fifty-six dollars was too much to come out of Mr. Nelson's pocket. It was not right for him to contribute to a prostitute who died from HIV. The truth was a lie and the lie was truth to him. At my funeral there were many people. Daphne and Carole came weeping over my soulless body as it reached the ground. I wasn't expecting anyone else but them.

Three months after my death, Christina went on to live with her father, Mr. Nelson. If you wondering about him, the orphanage gets donations every week. It has been that way since the orphanage started, yet the kids barely see the four hundred dollars coming in monthly. Carole works extra days at the farm to support the other kids. Mr. Nelson lives in his semimansion with his daughter, who's soon to attend one of the most expensive colleges in Haiti. Christina got part of what she always wanted—a rich lifestyle—and as for going to America, the journey still continues.

Entering the orphanage, I sense a different vibe, a different atmosphere than when I was alive. It's a good vibe; everyone smiles more often, forgetting the orphan label. The kids are not happy now because of my death, rather because Christina no longer lives in the house controlling what they do. After discovering she was the heir to the Nelson orphanage, she became more controlling of everything—what we ate, the amount of water we used to shower with—and of course Carole worked for her and only her. She even asked Carole to quit her job at the farm in order to make sure her chores were done for when she comes back from school. When it comes to the food, she had to give the okay on what Carole could cook. It would be unselfish of her if she complained to her father about the food that we ate overall, but no, according to her, Carole had to cook something different made only for her every single day while we ate rice and beans and hardened bread every day for the next few months. Living under her supervision was tough. That's one thing I don't miss about being alive, being told what to do by Christina. Under her father's care she demands assets and her ticket to America of course. Without Carole, I wonder how less easy things will be for her. Christina comes with chores, lots of it. Mr. Nelson, a man who had no one to look after prior to Christina, lacks skills to attend to her needs. She sees herself as a princess who's forbidden to care about anyone else but herself.

Nelson comes to the orphanage more than once a month now, begging Carole to do Christina's chores, which included washing and ironing her clothes, washing her school sneakers sometimes, even cooking her favorite food. He demanded Carole to keep her clothes separate from the rest of the kids. He was afraid that I left my HIV trace behind. The first time he came over with her clothes, she asked to be paid in order to do these lasting chores. "Christina no longer lives here, so why should I be doing her chores? If you want me to do anything for her, I demand you pay me." Carole told Mr. Nelson. He had threatened her with her job at the orphanage if she refused to do what she's told.

"You work for me, do you understand?"

"How about I quit right now, leaving you with more kids?"

"You pay me one hundred dollars a month to give care to fifteen kids. You and your daughter treat me with no respect, and now you come here demanding me to wash clothes for your kid who no longer lives here. The only reason I'm here is because of these kids. Not your pity money!"

"I'm sorry if I treat you wrong. All I'm saying is I can't wash her clothes, and she says she doesn't know how to. I believe her!"

"Mr. Nelson, let me tell you this. She is still injured from your news. She's a professional at manipulating people to get what she wants. She's done it to Jasmine, myself, and her colleagues. I'm afraid you're being manipulated by her. She is taking advantage of you. She washes her clothes every week when she used to live here. It wasn't until you showed up in the picture, her father, she stops doing her chores."

"I know she's still hurt, I'm trying to give her time to heal. She tells me she doesn't know how to, and I believe her. She told me you never liked her anyway. If you did you wouldn't be talking about her with such unpleasantness."

"If you think I'm going to wash these clothes I'd rather take all these kids and leave your orphanage."

"Where are you going to go? I'm the only thing you've got!" Nelson added.

"Oh really, you think so? These kids are what keeps me here. If it wasn't for them, I would've been long gone."

"Let's end this argument. How about I give you forty dollars to wash them?"

"Now you're talking. Don't be coming up in here thinking I'll still be doing Christina favors. Especially after what she did to Jasmine."

"What did she do to Jasmine? The prostitute died of HIV, that's not her fault. Don't pin this on my daughter."

"She could have lived for another month if your daughter didn't open her big mouth to the whole school."

No matter how much convincing anyone did to Mr. Nelson, he still maintained his position—I caught the deadly sexually transmitted disease from prostitution. I didn't like being called that for a bigger reason than that; it tears me up seeing my aunt Annabel doing such a degrading activity. What I hated most about being alive was what some people saw me as. Till this day it still hurts me that I couldn't change their minds about me. Carole maintains her position. Christina was the reason behind my shortened life. No, it wasn't because of her I died. Yes, the condition I died in could have been prevented. My time was up. The reason I didn't wake up dead on my bedside that morning was because I was holding on to someone who believes in my words. She believed that I wasn't a prostitute. I thought if I kept the warts, the blisters hidden well enough maybe I could have surpassed my seven months. Dr. Jean was correct when he told me seven months was my deadline. He knew well. I died seven months and three days later. There was no beating the odds. Three days extra was how long my body was able to withstand the capacity of the AIDS permeating my body.

"From now on you will not control the things the kids and I do in this orphanage. You have your daughter now. Just leave us alone. If you don't have anything good to say or give us, leave us be."

"Okay, whatever you want, Carole. You're now the woman of the house. As for Jasmine, let's forget about her. She's dead now."

"Let's forget about her? You never remembered her to begin with. Where's Christina anyway? You're losing her already."

"She's at the hair salon getting her hair done." A princess, she was getting to spend her father's worth. Being dead comes with many gifts; for example I can drop in anytime I want to at the orphanage, checking on everyone. Mr. Nelson still thinks I'm a prostitute, and Carole still reminds me of the mother I always missed.

Ryan gets her Carole back. He now goes to the park more often than usual with her, making friends, not worrying about growing up too fast or thinking of his disgraceful family who left him at the hospital. As he grew older though, he started wondering about their existence. Carole now had to predict these answers. My room was cleaned magnificently for him. He now sleeps in there by himself with a brand-new TV Carole bought for him with her own money. No statics if you're wondering. He watches his cartoons free of that. He is happy for now. Things are different now that I'm gone. Every minute of every hour Carole somehow finds her way to think of me. Ryan somehow fills that void.

Daphne goes to Harmony often. What she sees is no longer what I saw. She lays underneath the blue sky, wondering if I'm present, observing the same thing she sees, the images of the animals appearing in the clouds. A bridge with many memories is where she lays for comfort, hoping one day her old life will return for her. Her mother now works at the school cafeteria, making $1.50 an hour. As her struggle begins, one ends with the question of where will her afterlife take her.

Charlene still remains at Judem Valley High, inconspicuously waiting for the next rich girl who's going to pop into those doors and bring her to America. Her dream still remains as she mooches of the next one. A warm heart she needed. A true friend she wants. Julmina was capable of giving her all of that. Julmina was her ticket to America. Still, she keeps looking in the wrong direction. She was worth all that she wanted. Julmina was only the shadow that kept her organized. If she looks at her differently rather than the girl who carried her books to class, things could change and so would her cold heart. A different look is all she needs.

As for me, watching Annabel is my mission. My soul cannot settle until she's removed from this paralyzing atmosphere. Watching her waste her life deprived me. If one man who raped me left me ill, what happens to her then? Could she also be dealing with the disease that stole my life from me? She sleeps with men of different kinds—old, young, and the promiscuous. Often when I look at her in disguise I see a sick individual who now needed my help. As I once needed help, it was my turn now to offer aid to someone else, someone dearest to my mother.

To some people she might be ugly; to one specific man, she's beautiful. Behind those sunken eyes, Adam Laxford saw an amazing woman destined to be his wife. He's been praising her for years, but she sees him differently. A man with such heavy pockets offers to end her misery but she refuses. To her, he was another man paying for sexual favors even when he showed no signs of such thing. "I'm taking you home with me today," Adam says to her.

"How many times do I have to tell you I don't go to people's houses? Do you have a car?"

"I have a limo that's willing to drive you anywhere you want."

"How much do you have?" she asked him.

"I want to help you, Annabel. That's the only thing I want from you."

"I don't need your help. Don't you see I'm making my own money my own way?"

"This way can get you killed. The possibilities of you getting diseases from these people are at high risk, my friend."

"If you're looking for money, I have none."

"You could use a nice shower," he says to her.

"Yeah, I could use that." She sniffles.

"Then come with me."

"I will provide you with anything you need."

"What's the catch? I've told you I have no money."

"Nothing. I just want you to stop doing this. You don't have to make your money this way."

"It's the only way I know how to."

"Come with me. I will show you other ways."

"I don't have anywhere else to go after that."

"You can stay with me till whenever you need to."

Annabel lives a successful life, free of diseases. She now has two wonderful boys who live like princes. She has a happy husband who has forgotten the dark path she underwent. With a princess in the way, her life is now complete. She travels the world with her family by her side just like she one day wished for. Dreams do come true, even when you feel disappointed in yourself. All you need is genuine love to lift you up.

Harmony still remains my place of peace. Near Daphne is where I invisibly lay, underneath the blue sky, admiring what heaven has created. My mom lives blissfully with God. I often take trips down to Joule Ville to remember the woman that made me strong. Carole was the oman who gracefully sees me as her child, cared for me as one of her own. She smiles and my day is brighter. She lives her life under no one's authority. She makes her own rules along with fifteen other kids. The bridge that I often call another home still remains the place for harmony to Daphne still has the same values as it did for me when I was alive. Love was what I spent most of my life searching for; love is now what I have finally found underneath the skies and above the skies.

I'm not complaining about the life I have now, but if I had my way I would have chosen differently. In a line amongst ambitious peers is where I had hoped to be, graduating at the top of my class. If I had my way my father wouldn't exist only in my imagination, my mother would have lived beyond her years, my aunt wouldn't even have known about drugs, and I would be an educated woman striving to achieve her dreams. If I could have my way, the world wouldn't be able to handle Jasmine Pierce, the ambitious and indestructible young woman. Sad part about my life is, I didn't get a chance to get my way. It's okay though. Maybe someone else who has gone through a similar agony will be able to achieve their goals.

As I look across the town that has captured my life and isolated my grieving, I had a quick flashback of the faceless man. This time I wasn't running away from him. I saw a man begging for clemency.

It was that one flashback that assured me that I had finally gotten my wish. Alive, I can only describe my experience as a being as "taken." Now I can only describe myself and my experience so far in my afterlife as merciful. I am merciful because I no longer live in anguish. With a new soul I stand cured; cured from a disease that my kind has determined was incurable. I proved them wrong! If only they can see now how better I am, how good I feel, they would reconsider their assumption of life after HIV. It's not sudden death, its throwing out the old flesh and receiving a new soul.

My father still remains a mystery. I have given up on the search of finding him. I have realized now that he doesn't want to be found. Finding him would have given me the answers that I needed. It bothered me throughout the days of my life, but now not so much anymore. Occasionally I find myself thinking of a man that I have never seen, only in a picture that I've created in my head, my hopeful imagination. It's okay if I never get to see what he really looks like. I'm strong, and I'm getting even stronger now with or without knowing him. My name is Jasmine Pierce. I am twenty years old, and even though I've longed for the truth about my father. I am not forgotten, for it is his lonely existence that is forgotten.

I spent my whole life being defined by my appearance, by a disease that took over my entire life. Now that it's over, I really don't know what's next. I hadn't really planned my afterlife as my mother had planned my life. I had never really thought of what would be next for me except for the part that was going get erased from the place that taunted me. One thing that I know for sure here is that I will never have to live my life in fear. Fear of an unidentified man constantly chasing me or in fear of my surroundings, hoping to see sadness and despair in my deep brown eyes. There's nothing left to do now but enjoy what my afterlife has to offer. I'm leaving this forsaken town behind for those who truly deserve it. To people like Christina and Charlene who care for nothing but themselves, I'm leaving this town to the narcissistic, and I am never looking back. I never thought I would say this, but I have nowhere to go. I feel like I have a new world in the palm of my hands just waiting for me to choose a destination. I am Jasmine Pierce, and I was born on this bright Sunday morning at twelve o'clock, free of obstacles. New life, good health, and a fresh start!